HEAR

THEM

SCREAM

Kristen Middleton

NY Times and USA Today Bestselling Author

MIDDLETON

Fantasy, Horror, and Romance.

BOOKS BY KRISTEN MIDDLETON

SEARCHING FOR FAITH
LOOKING FOR LAINEY
FORGET ME NOT
HEAR THEM SCREAM

BLUR
SHIVER
VENGEANCE
ILLUSIONS

VENOM
SLADE
TOXIC
CLAIMED BY THE LYCAN

JEZEBEL

HEAR THEM SCREAM

DEVIANT

ENCHANTED SECRETS
ENCHANTED OBJECTS
ENCHANTED SPELLS

ORIGINS
RUNNING WILD
DEAD ENDZ
ROAD KILL
END ZONE

PAXTON VS THE UNDEAD

PLANET Z
BLOOD OF BREKKON

ROMANCE UNDER PEN NAME K.L. MIDDLETON

TANGLED BEAUTY
TANGLED MESS
TANGLED FURY

SHARP EDGES

BILLIONAIRE AT SEA
BILLIONAIRE AT SEA BOOK 2

GRITTY BIKER ROMANCE UNDER PEN NAME CASSIE ALEXANDRA

RESISTING THE BIKER
SURVIVING THE BIKER
FEARING THE BIKER
BREAKING THE BIKER
TAMING THE BIKER
LOVING THE BIKER
LURING THE BIKER
CHRISTMAS WITH THE BIKER
DESTROYING THE BIKER
TAUNTING THE BIKER

Chapter 1

Sunday, October 15th
1:20 a.m.
Top Shelf Saloon
Bear Creek, Minnesota

The Director

"GO TO HELL, Tommy," the blonde snapped before tossing what was left of her beer at the tall, tattooed Neanderthal she'd entered the bar with earlier. Nobody would have guessed that just twenty-minutes before, she'd been sitting on his lap, giggling and flirting with the dirt-bag.

And me.

Although we'd never met, I'd caught her staring and smiling my way a few times. Of course, I'd encouraged it by grinning back. Not because I was attracted to her. She just had what I needed.

"You, bitch!" he growled, shooting up out of his chair. He raised his hand to backhand her when the bouncer, Leo, who'd been monitoring the couple's argument, made his move.

"I wasn't going to hit her," Tommy lied as Leo grabbed his elbow and shoved him away from the table.

"You're going to have to leave," Leo said sternly. Although he was shorter than Tommy, the bouncer was twice as muscular and wore a patched vest that identified him as a member of a notorious outlaw biker club, the *Jersey Rebels*. Everyone knew that screwing with Leo meant trouble.

Tommy began to protest. "I didn't do anything. She's the one who threw the damn beer at me."

"From where I was standing, you deserved it," Leo replied. "Now, either you walk out on your own, or I can escort you. It's your choice."

Sulking, Tommy called Amber a few names before grabbing his leather jacket, and walking toward the doorway. He turned around at the last minute and told her to have fun walking home in the dark.

She flipped him off with both middle fingers.

Giving it to her right back, Tommy left in a huff.

"You okay?" Leo asked her.

She nodded.

"You need a ride home?"

Amber shook her head. "Nah. I only live a couple of blocks from here. I'll be fine. Thanks, though."

Leo reminded her that a lot could happen in a couple of blocks.

She groaned. "Why does everyone think I need a *man* to protect me? I can take care of myself."

He shrugged. "Suit yourself. Just trying to be nice."

"Yeah, right. I've learned that nice comes with a price and I'm sick of paying. From now on, Amber Simons—" she jerked her thumb toward her chest— "isn't falling for any more bullshit. So, thanks... but no thanks."

The bouncer rolled his eyes.

I had to admit, she had spunk. The woman was exactly what I was looking for.

Amber's phone went off. She glanced at the screen, scowled, and shoved it into an oversized, fringy black leather purse. Grabbing what was left of Tommy's beer, she slammed it down, stood up, and walked toward the ladies' room. A few minutes later, she came back out and headed toward the front door.

"If Tommy comes back, tell him to kiss my ass, Leo!" she called out.

The bouncer, who was helping to clean up a spill at the bar, waved without looking. "Will do. See ya!"

I finished off my beer, put my cowboy hat on, and followed her outside into the brisk, early October morning. She wasn't dressed for the weather with her thin, black jacket and jean mini skirt. In fact, she was already shivering. I knew this was going to be easy.

Hearing the door shut behind me, Amber turned from where she was standing by the cigarette-butt pail. She relaxed when she saw it was me.

"Evenin'. I mean… mornin'," I said, giving her a lopsided grin and titling my hat. "Gotta love this weather, huh? It's cold enough out here to freeze the balls off of a pool table."

Amber's eyes shined with amusement. "You've got that right." She looked down at my light-blue jean jacket and matching Levis. "You're not from around here, are you?"

"Nope. Afraid not."

"I didn't think so. I'd have remembered you." She leaned back against the building. "You from Texas?"

That night, I was.

I curled my thumbs through the loops of my jeans and rocked back and forth on my boots. "Originally. I'm living in San Diego now."

"Oh, yeah? What are you doing here in Minnesota?" she asked, pulling a pack of cigarettes out of her jacket pocket.

Time for the HOOK.

"I'm here for business," I explained, which was partially true. I was in Bear Creek for something a little bit more.

9

"Oh? What do you do?"

"I'm a casting director."

Her eyebrow arched. "For what? Commercials?"

"No, movies."

Amber smiled. "Wow, that's really cool. As in the Hollywood kind?"

I nodded.

"No offense, but I thought maybe you were here for a rodeo or something. Then I remembered—it's almost winter time and those usually happen in the summer around here," she said, brushing a blonde curl away from her eyes.

I smiled. "Actually, I don't always dress like this," I said, sweeping my arm down. "I'm usually in a tie or one of those monkey suits."

"I bet you look mighty fine in a monkey suit," she replied, looking me over with approval.

I cupped my hand behind my ear.

She gave me a funny look. "What's wrong? You hear something?"

"I'm waiting for the sirens. Something tells me there's going to be a warrant out for your arrest," I grinned, "stealing my heart like that. You're a dangerous woman."

She laughed and shook her head. "Oh, Lord."

"Too much?" I asked, chuckling.

"No, actually, I was just thinking that some things are worth going to prison for," she replied, batting her eyelashes at me.

"Couldn't agree with you more."

"You want a smoke?" she asked, holding out her pack of Newport cigarettes.

"No, thank you. I quit a while ago."

She lit the end of hers and took a drag. "I wish I could. Nights like this make it hard."

I stared off toward the parking lot, wondering if her meathead boyfriend was lurking around. "I'm sure. Who was the asshole?"

"Tommy?" She rolled her eyes. "Just this guy I've been dating. He's an asshole, alright. Always jealous as hell."

"Is that right?"

Amber smiled slowly. "Yep. Tonight he was angry about you."

"Me? Why is that?"

"I think he may have caught me checking you out. It was all in innocence, of course. But, Tommy freaked out and actually accused me of acting like a whore." She frowned and took a drag of her smoke. "The prick."

"He's definitely not worth your time."

Amber sighed. "Yeah. I've been telling myself that for the last few weeks."

"A girl like you should be treasured, and for him to treat you with such little respect is deplorable. You're obviously much too good for a loser like him."

She grinned.

LINE.

"I swear to God, your smile just made the temperature go up about twenty degrees," I flirted.

"Right," she replied, still smiling. "You're so full of it."

"No, seriously," I took off my jean jacket. "I'm getting too warm over here."

"I'm freezing my ass off."

"I see that," I said, noticing her teeth were beginning to chatter. "Here." I held it out to her. "You should put it on. You'll catch yourself a cold out here."

"That's so sweet of you. I couldn't take your jacket, though."

"Nonsense. Please. Warm yourself up."

Amber put her cigarette out. "Fine, if you insist on being such a perfect gentleman, I can at least make the effort worthwhile." She put the jacket over her shoulders and stared at the black Johnny Cash T-shirt I had on. "So, you're into old country music?"

SINKER.

"Yes, I enjoy classical and jazz, too. I'm also into old art, old movies, and good, old-fashioned manners.

12

Especially around beautiful women. Now, *that* never gets old."

She chuckled. "And you call *me* dangerous? You really are a charmer, aren't you?"

This time I gave *her* an appraising look. "Just trying to be on my best behavior around a pretty girl."

"You're not so bad looking yourself. I'm surprised you're not in the movies, instead of casting roles."

"My mother was the actress of the family," I said, my smile leaving.

"Really? What's her name?"

I told her.

"Huh. Sorry, I've never heard of her," Amber replied.

I shrugged. "She was mostly in 'B' movies. Horror ones."

"Was? She died?"

I nodded.

"Sorry for your loss."

I wasn't.

One of the highlights of my life had been watching the bitch die. I could still remember the shock in her eyes as I choked the last breath out of her scrawny neck. She'd always thought of me as a coward. Had mocked and ridiculed me about it to no end. I showed her just how wrong she'd been and it had been me who'd had the last laugh.

13

"It's getting cold out here. You need a ride home?" I asked, worried that someone would soon see us together. This was taking too long.

She stared at me and chewed on her lower lip. "You're not some kind of a psycho trying to bring me home so you can chop me up into little pieces, are you?"

I laughed. "Damn, you're not only beautiful, but a psychic. Let's drive to Vegas. We'll get hitched and win ourselves a fortune."

She laughed. "Right."

I gave her a serious look. "In all honesty, I was thinking that your boyfriend might be waiting for you at home. You shouldn't have to deal with that tonight."

Amber frowned. "Yeah, He's been texting me left and right. He's probably at my doorstep right now."

"You're welcome to come back to the house I'm renting. It's not far from here. We can have a drink and then when it's safe, I'll bring you home. Or, you can sleep in my guestroom."

Her eyes roved over me and she nodded. "I guess you look harmless enough. Just so you know, I'm not easy. So, if you're thinking about getting lucky, you're wasting your time."

"I'm not easy either." I winked. "My mama always told me to go slow and treat a woman like a lady."

"Your momma sounds like a wise woman. I bet she had a big ol' heart, huh?"

A big, ol' empty one.

"Speaking of bigger, they say everything is bigger in Texas," Amber flirted. "Is that a bunch of B.S. or the honest to goodness truth?"

"I can't answer that 'cause it would be braggin' and Mama taught me never to do that either."

She let out a breathy sigh. "Where's your ride?

TWENTY MINUTES LATER, we'd barely made it through my front door and she was all over me.

"Cowboy, I want you so badly. It almost hurts," she groaned against my mouth, her hands everywhere.

I wanted her, too.

And there'd definitely be some pain involved.

"Amber," I whispered, pulling back slightly.

"What?"

I stared into her eyes, imagining them filled with terror. It was enough to get the blood flowing in every direction. "How hard can you scream?"

She gave me a funny look and smiled. "That depends," she said, reaching for my fly. "On what you plan to do to me."

I grabbed her wrist firmly. "Now, that's exactly what I wanted to hear."

"PLEASE, LET ME go!" Amber begged over Fred Astaire's melodic voice as he sang *Cheek to Cheek*. It was just one of many classical songs that really put me in the mood.

"I hope you're not too cold," I said, staring down at her as she writhed around on the gurney. She was naked with her ankles and wrists tethered to the corner posts. I had to admit, unclothed she was a little disappointing, especially with the rose and dagger tattoo on her hip. I'd wanted virgin skin for the scene we were going to shoot. In the original film, which had been released back in '73, the woman had pale, flawless skin. Now I knew that to recreate it, I would need to use stage makeup on Amber. Not a big deal, but it would take some extra time.

"You freak! Let me go!" she demanded, glaring at me. "Now!"

Ignoring her ramblings, I wheeled my three camera stands around the room, one by one, to get the best angles and then adjusted the lighting until I was satisfied. Meanwhile, Amber continued swearing and calling me every name imaginable, which put a smile on my face. She was a spitfire. Tattoos, or not, I'd definitely found myself the right actress.

"The camera is going to love you. You're a natural."

"Camera? You're going to be videotaping me?"

"Yes. Have you ever seen the movie, *I'm Still Breathing?*'"

She didn't reply.

"It was a film about a woman injected with some kind of experimental drug by the government to make a few bucks. She panicked and left the facilities only to pass out in an alley. When she came to, she was being prepped for an autopsy. You see, the drug she'd been injected with caused her heart and pulse to slow so much, everyone thought she'd died. Of course, the drug didn't wear off until it was too late and so she had to endure the terror and pain of the procedure. Anyway, I'm going to try a concoction I've been experimenting with, using Liquid X and Rohypnol. I didn't get it quite right, the last time, but I feel pretty confident about this newest mixture."

She stared at me in horror.

I grinned. "So, you *have* seen it?"

Pulling at her restraints, Amber began to cry. "Why are you doing this?"

"Number one, it's fun. Number two, other people enjoy my movies. Number three," I grinned again, "I can't seem to stop."

"Butchering people is *fun?* What kind of a monster are you?"

I snapped my finger. "Oh, yeah, I'm also doing this for my mother, God rest her soul. You see, she actually played the female lead in *I'm Still Breathing*,

17

and her birthday is tomorrow. I thought it would be a nice tribute to her. Which reminds me, I almost forgot the perfume."

I reached into my tool bag and pulled out the bottle of Chanel No 5. It had been my mother's favorite and I used it on all of my actresses. I sprayed some on Amber, who began to cry again.

"Please, let me go…" she sobbed.

I ignored her. "Do you like movies? I've always been a fan of horror movies, which is why I love recreating them. Not to mention, people are willing to pay an arm and a leg to see them. And… be in them." I chuckled at my own joke.

"You're insane."

I walked over to the cameras and switched them on. "Maybe. Maybe not. Like Mother used to say, 'Embrace your flaws. They are what make you perfect, in an imperfect world.'"

"Please."

I pulled the surgical mask over my mouth and then wheeled the medical tool stand next to her.

Seeing the sharp objects, she tried fighting against the restraints. "If you let me go, I'll do anything you want!" she pleaded. "Just tell me what I need to do!"

I picked up the scalpel, breathed on it, and wiped off an irritating smudge. "You know what I want? Your screams, Amber. Just like how a burp is a natural sign of a good meal, a scream is a natural

18

response to terror." Smiling, I brought the knife to her nipple. "So, darlin', don't hold back."

Fortunately, she did not disappoint…

Chapter 2

Friday, October 20th,
8:45 pm

Whitney

"WHIT, YOU ARE *not* backing out of this trip," my twin sister, Brittany, said from her end of the phone. "The cabin is already booked and you have no idea what it took for me to get this time off from work. We're so understaffed right now, it's ridiculous."

"I know. I know. I'm not trying to be a pain, I just can't get up there until Tuesday. I *have* to be in court on Monday. We're in the middle of this important case and Jack needs me there. I'm free the rest of the week, though. I promise."

I was a paralegal for a busy law firm and Brittany, my twin, was a nurse. We were both twenty-seven, single, and living in Michigan, two hundred miles away from each other. Since our schedules were crazy, and we didn't get to see each other very often, we managed to take an annual trip together. Usually, it was in the summer, but this year we were going to visit our Uncle Rocky in Summit Lake, Minnesota. Although he'd offered to let us stay with him and his wife, Jan, we ended up booking a lovely cabin on the lake.

She let out a long sigh. "Fine. I guess there's nothing we can do about it. But, if you *dare* call me Monday night and cancel for the rest of the week, I'm going to sneak into your condo and wrinkle every piece of clothing you own."

"Seriously, that doesn't bother me anymore," I lied, wishing she'd forgotten about my neurotic obsession. I knew it was weird, but I couldn't leave the house in anything that wasn't perfectly pressed. Nor, could I sleep comfortably in wrinkled pajamas. I ironed everything, even my sheets if they came out of the dryer wrinkled. One morning I was even late to work because of my phobia. I'd made it to the parking lot and had noticed a couple of irritating wrinkles on my blouse. The anxiety had been too much so I drove home, ironed it, and clocked in forty minutes late. Brittany claimed that it was some kind of "comfort mechanism" I'd created for myself.

She ignored me and kept talking. "Seriously, test me and I *will* replace all of your clothing with items made of linen."

"You bitch," I replied, amused.

"Damn straight." Brittany chuckled. "Not to mention, I'm wrinkle free. That's why you love me."

I smiled. "You goof. Anyway, I promise. I'll be there. You have my word."

"I hope so. Uncle Rocky and Jan are excited to see you, too."

"Have you talked to him lately?" I asked.

He was a retired paramedic, who'd married later in life. Although he never had children, Britt and I agreed that he would have made a wonderful father. Fortunately, his wife's daughter, Amanda, had a young son who adored him and called him Grandpa. He was also our favorite uncle, and although he was a little rough around the edges, Rocky had a heart of gold.

"Actually, I spoke to him last night. Apparently, he's made some special plans for us," she mused.

"Like what?"

"He mentioned buying tickets for this ghostly dinner cruise. It's supposed to take us to this scary haunted Canyon. Jan refused to go, so it will just be the three of us."

It sounded like fun. "Is it really supposed to be haunted?"

"Who knows? I think it will be a blast, though. I haven't been to a haunted house, or anything scary like that, in ages."

Neither had I. "Are you still planning on driving to Summit Lake instead of flying?" I asked.

"Yeah. I'm leaving in the morning. Hopefully around six, if I can get my butt out of bed."

If everything went as planned, she'd get up there around four p.m.

"What about you? Are you driving or flying?" she asked.

"Driving. In fact, I was thinking about leaving Monday night. Right after work."

"After work? You'd be on the road all night. You'll fall asleep," she said.

"If I get tired, I'll stop at a motel. I just want to get out there as quickly as I can."

"*You* should actually take an airplane."

"And miss the scenic route? It should be a gorgeous drive."

Autumn was my favorite time of the year. I loved sweater-weather, the colorful leaves, and the smell of bonfires. Unfortunately, it never lasted long enough and we both knew that the snow could come any day. Even in October.

"I'm looking forward to it, too," she said. "That's really the only reason why I'm driving."

I crawled onto my bed and stared up at the light fixture on my ceiling. There was a small shadow inside of it and I wondered if it was a spider. Ugh, I really hated spiders. "Have you talked to Dad lately?" I asked, getting back off the mattress.

"No. The last I heard, he was taking Lillian to the French Riviera because of some fashion show she wanted to see."

I rolled my eyes. Lillian was his girlfriend and twenty-five years younger. Not much older than us, in fact. Britt and I didn't care for her and considered the woman nothing but a gold-digger. Our father owned a Mercedes dealership and Lillian had started out in his life as a receptionist there, but now owned two fancy cars and apparently, his heart. She obviously had him wrapped around her little finger.

"They haven't gotten engaged yet, have they?" I asked.

"Not that I'm aware of. You should give him a call. He thinks you're angry with him."

"I *am* angry," I replied, pulling out my vacuum cleaner from the hallway closet. "He used to preach about being smart with your heart and now he's being ignorant, allowing himself to be bamboozled by Lillian."

"I don't know if he's as naïve about her as you believe. Anyway, he's enjoying himself, so what's the harm?"

24

I dragged the vacuum back into my bedroom. "I just don't want to see him hurt. I understand having a midlife crisis, but my gut is telling me that she's trouble."

"Because of Vinnie?"

Vinnie was Lillian's ex-boyfriend. I'd seen the two a few weeks ago leaving a restaurant together. I'd brought it up to our father, who claimed to have known about it. According to Dad, Vinnie and Lillian had met as "friends" and there wasn't anything personal between them anymore. That they'd ended their romantic relationship years ago.

Well, I wasn't buying into that B.S.

Especially after finding out that Vinnie was an ex-con who'd gone to prison for eight years after swindling money from innocent people. Apparently, he'd borrowed thousands of dollars from some local women he'd "friended" through social media. He took them out on dates and, eventually, persuaded the women into writing checks for fake investments. Fortunately, it caught up with him and Vinnie did some time. My concern was that he was now working with Lillian to swindle our father out of money.

I leaned down and plugged the vacuum into my wall.

"Yes, because of that creep."

"Dad's not gullible. He's just lonely and wants a beautiful woman on his arm. If something seems shady with Lillian, he's going to figure it out."

"Let's hope so," I replied, not so sure.

"Call him, Whit."

I sighed. "Yeah, I will."

We spoke for a few more minutes and then she told me she had some errands to run.

"I can't wait to see you," Brittany said. "It seems like it's been forever."

It had actually been three months and I felt the same way. Being twins, of course we were close, although it hadn't always been the case. There'd been a time, back in high school, when we'd barely been on speaking terms. All because of a boy.

Samuel Lancaster.

The three of us grew up together and had lived on the same street. From the time I'd been little, I'd always had a secret crush on him, as did a lot of the girls in our school. Samuel had been the classic tall, dark, and handsome soccer player with a smile that made you blush and eyes that haunted your dreams. He'd had plenty of girlfriends, although he'd flirted constantly with Britt, the more social and outgoing of the two of us. As much as we looked alike, our personalities had always been like night-and-day. Especially back in those days. Where I'd been the serious one, Brittany had been the partying, reckless twin who'd managed to set trends and earn homecoming crowns. Samuel used to say it was our differences that made us so interesting and fun to be around.

Especially to him, apparently.

One time, back in the eleventh grade, Samuel and I went canoeing together, alone, because Brittany had been stuck working that particular day. Once we were on the lake, Samuel had pulled out a bottle of peach Schnapps and offered me some. Although I'd been to parties before where alcohol flowed freely, I wasn't one to indulge. That time, however, I accepted because it had been Samuel offering, and… I didn't want him to think of me as being lame. Of course, we both became tipsy and somehow ended up making out. Afterward, when we were in his car and had shared more of the Schnapps, Samuel tried going further with me—much more than I'd wanted to. In fact, at one point I'd almost had to fight him off. Angry, and accusing me of being a tease, he brought me home, making me doubt myself and wondering if I *had* somehow led him on. Later that night, I told my sister about it. Instead of being upset for me, she became jealous, stating that the two of them had started dating recently and swore she'd told me about it.

"Why would you let him kiss you when you knew we were seeing each other?" she'd asked, angrily.

27

"First of all, I didn't know, otherwise I wouldn't have *ever* kissed him back. Second of all, he tried raping me, Britt. Doesn't that mean anything to you?"

Unfortunately, she'd been so resentful that she couldn't see beyond the fact that I'd shared a bottle of Schnapps and made out with her boyfriend. Then, when she confronted Samuel about it, he admitted to getting drunk and acting stupid, but swore he never forced himself on me. By that time, everything seemed like one big blur and I even questioned my own actions that day. In the end, she did break up with Samuel, but it put a ripple in our relationship. One that lasted until college. It wasn't until our mother became terminally ill that we hashed things out, putting the past behind us. I learned that Britt had been carrying around the guilt of not supporting me when I'd needed her the most. As for me, I realized that Samuel's accusations had been meaningless. No matter what had happened, when I said 'no', he should have backed off.

"It does seem like it's been forever," I replied. "And, I'm looking forward to the trip, too. By the way, call or text me when you get to Summit Lake. So I know you made it there safely."

"Will do," she replied. "And you be careful yourself. Don't push yourself to drive all night, just to get out here. I'd rather have you safe thea lying in a hospital bed because you fell asleep at the wheel."

"Point taken."

"Good. Love ya."

I smiled. "Love you, too."

Chapter 3

Whitney

AFTER HANGING UP with Brittany, I vacuumed up the spider, made myself some popcorn, and watched a couple of older episodes of *This Is Us.* Afterward, I went back into the bedroom and put on a pair of flannel pajamas. Noticing that they were wrinkled, I tried not to let it bother me, but ended up breaking out the iron. Once I was finished pressing them, I put my pajamas back on and sighed. Although the smell of freshly steamed cotton was comforting, my obsession with ironing things *had* to end.

It wasn't normal.

I decided that as soon as I returned home from Summit Lake, I would schedule an appointment with a hypnotist. If they were able to assist smokers, hopefully they could help iron out my problems, too.

THE NEXT MORNING, I rolled out of bed at seven, took a shower, pulled my hair up into a messy bun, threw on a pair of jeggings, along with a mauve V-neck sweater, and went into the office to do some last minute research for the upcoming trial. While I was finishing up, Jack Wagner, one of the attorneys I worked for, walked into the main lobby. Noticing me at my desk, he grinned and walked over.

"Hey, Jack, I didn't know you were stopping in today," I said, wishing I would have sped things up and left before he'd arrived.

"I forgot something in my office." He moved closer and sat down on the corner of my desk. "I also figured I'd see if you wanted to join me for lunch."

I gathered the stack of paperwork in front of me and stood up. "Sorry. I can't."

"Hey, it would just a friendly bite to eat. Nothing more."

I moved around him and headed toward the copy machine. "If you want to have lunch with a friend, you have plenty to choose from."

Sighing, he followed me over. "Aren't you ever going to forgive me? I told you it meant nothing."

He was talking about a kiss I'd seen him share with one of his clients a month ago. I'd walked into his office, thinking he was alone, and caught Jack lip-locked with a woman he was representing in a divorce case. He'd claimed that she'd instigated it and had caught him off guard at the precise moment I'd entered the room. Whether it was true or not, from where I'd been standing, he'd been enjoying it.

"I don't want to talk about it anymore. We've been back-and-forth about this so much," I replied, putting the stack of paper into the feed. "It's exhausting."

"But I miss you," he pouted, reaching over and tugging on a lock of my hair. "I miss us."

I had a feeling it was the quickies in the office he missed more than anything. The truth was, we'd had a whirlwind romance, one that had been more physical than anything. Admittedly, I still had some feelings for him, which was why I couldn't seem to put in my two-week notice. But I wanted more, and I knew deep inside that he didn't.

"I'm sorry," I replied, stepping back. "But, I'd rather keep our relationship platonic. It's better this way."

He frowned. "Is there someone else?"

"Not at the moment. Now," I handed him the copies. "Here's the list of assets for the Butlers. Is there anything else you need before I leave for the day?"

He pursed his lips together. "Yeah, but obviously you're still holding a grudge, so it's not going to happen. I may as well open up that bottle of Cristal I purchased earlier and drink my sorrows away."

I shook my head and smiled coolly. I'd mentioned to him a couple of weeks ago that I'd always wanted to try the champagne, but refused to pay the hefty price-tag myself. "Don't be so dramatic, Jack."

"Don't be so stubborn," he replied, trying to grab my hand. "Whit—"

"Enough," I said firmly, snaking my wrist away from him. "It's over."

"But, I can't bear to see you every day like this and not get to touch you. It's torture."

"That's not my problem. You know, if it's really going to bother you that much, maybe I should just look for a new job." I was beginning to think that it would be better for my own sanity, too. My heart and body wanted to give in to him so damn badly, but my mind knew better.

Sighing, he put the paperwork under his arm, turned around, and headed toward his office. "Now who's being dramatic?"

Whatever.

"Do you still need me for the trial on Monday?" I called out, ignoring the dig.

He looked back at me. "Why, are you planning on scouting for a new job?"

I almost bit my tongue to keep from saying something snippy back to him. "I'm supposed to meet my sister in Summit Lake, remember?"

Jack sighed. "That's right. Your 'annual trip'. Because I'm not the complete asshole you take me for, I'll handle Monday alone."

My eyes widened in surprise. "Really?"

"Yes. I know you've been looking forward to going. Besides, you work too hard as it is. Go and relax."

I smiled at him. "Thanks, Jack."

"You're welcome. I think some fresh air and rest is just what you need to clear your head. Maybe, afterward, you'll realize you can't live without me."

Or that I needed to get him out of my life permanently, I mused to myself.

"No comment on that?" he asked dryly.

"I know when to keep my mouth shut around a lawyer," I said with a smirk. "Thanks again, Jack."

"You bet. Be careful driving and say 'hello' to your family for me."

"I will," I replied, meaning just the driving part. My family didn't know about him, nor did they need to. As far as I was concerned, there was no future for us.

For once… it was a man I needed to iron out of my life, and it actually felt right.

Chapter 4

Whitney

AS SOON AS I got into my car, I called Brittany, who was still on the road. When she answered, I could hear Kelly Clarkson singing in the background. I told her the good news about leaving earlier than expected.

She squealed and lowered the volume of the music. "Yaay! What time are you going to start driving up here?"

I glanced at the clock. It was almost twelve; I still had to pick up my dry-cleaning, do a load of laundry, and not to mention, pack. The ironing could wait, considering that all of my clothing would be wrinkled by the time I got to Summit Lake, anyway. "Probably around four."

"Wait, so, you're *still* going to be driving at night?" She sighed. "Why don't you just leave in the morning? If you drive all night, you're going to sleep the day away tomorrow anyway."

She had a point. "Okay, I'll leave around four a.m. and hopefully get up there around dinner time."

"Sounds better. I'll pick up something to make on the barbecue for us, unless you'd rather go out to eat?"

"Whatever you want to do," I replied, although barbecue sounded wonderful. Living in an apartment, I didn't grill much. Mainly, because, it seemed like too much work for one person.

"Okay. I'll check the weather forecast and decide. I'm kind of in the mood for grilled chicken, myself."

"Yes, that sounds good. How's the drive been so far?"

"Very nice. The moment I drove out of the city, I could feel the stress begin to melt away," she said with a smile in her voice.

"Good. I'm looking forward to getting out of town myself. I still have a hard time believing I don't have to be in court on Monday. I keep waiting for Jack to call me and rescind his offer."

"Do you think he would do that?"

"No, but if he does… I'm quitting."

"You sound so serious when you say that," she mused.

She had no idea. The more I thought about it, the more I wanted to wash my hands of the guy.

"By the way, did you talk to Dad yet?"

I closed my eyes. I knew she'd ask. Brittany didn't like tension in the family. "I'm calling him on the way up, tomorrow."

"You'd better," she warned.

"I will. Don't worry."

We talked a little more and then I reminded her to call me when she made it to the cabin.

"Will do. By the way, Rocky said they were filming a movie in Summit Lake. Exciting, huh?"

The quaint little town was getting to be one of Minnesota's largest fishing and tourist destinations, especially with its numerous cabin resorts, Bed & Breakfasts, souvenir shops, and historical sites. So, it wasn't much of a surprise that a film was being made there.

"Really? That sounds interesting. Did he say who was in it or what it was about?"

"He wasn't sure, but heard that it was going to be a horror flick. I wonder if we can watch them film some of the movie?"

"It's probably a closed set, but you never know. I'm sure we'll run into someone working on the movie at one point." I smirked. "Maybe you could sweet-talk them into giving us a tour?"

"Now you're thinking," she said with a smile in her voice. "Oh, I see a gas station coming up. I need to refill and get myself a coffee. I'll call you later."

"Okay."

ON THE WAY home from the dry-cleaners, I stopped at Panera and purchased a cup of soup and a small Caesar salad. Once I reached my apartment, I threw in a load of laundry and ate my lunch. As I was finishing up, my cell phone rang.

It was Brittany again.

"What's up? You can't be there already," I said.

"Oh, my God, you'll never guess… Rocky just called to say that a woman's body was found in Bear Creek early this morning," she said in one long breath. "She was murdered."

My heart skipped a beat. That was too close to Summit Lake. Only forty-five minutes north of Uncle Rocky's house. "Wow. You're kidding? That's horrible. Do they have any idea of who she was or who did it?"

"The information hasn't been released yet. Rocky is good friends with the local Sheriff in Summit Lake, which is how he heard about it already. Anyway, some hikers found her in the woods. Can you imagine?"

"No. How scary. Well, hopefully they catch this person quickly."

"Yeah. Let's hope so. Remember that incident the year before, with Jan's daughter, Amanda?"

"Yeah."

She and her son, Kevin, had been through an ordeal that nearly cost them their lives. They'd been terrorized by some lunatic who'd had it out for Amanda, blaming her for things that had been beyond her control. I knew that moving past the nightmare couldn't have been easy. Especially for Kevin.

"What's going on with these small towns? I used to think it would be fun to retire in Summit Lake someday, but now... I'm not so sure," she muttered.

"People get murdered all the time in the large cities, too. It's just bigger news because it happened out there."

"I suppose you're right."

"If you hear anything else, let me know. And, for God's sake, be careful."

"You, too," she replied.

AFTER HANGING UP, I turned on the news, but didn't find anything about the murdered woman in Bear Creek. Hoping that they'd catch the killer soon, I made a mental note to call Rocky myself and get the scoop. Hopefully, they had a suspect or would arrest someone soon.

I spent the rest of the day preparing for the trip, and around five p.m., decided to watch another episode of *This Is Us*. I curled up onto the couch, fell asleep during the show, and didn't wake up until seven. Yawning, I picked my cell phone up and checked the messages, to see if I'd missed Brittany's call. I knew she should have already made it up to Summit Lake.

There was nothing.

Slightly worried, I called her.

She answered on the third ring.

"Is everything okay?" I asked.

"Yeah. I'm sorry. I totally forgot to call you," she replied, sounding winded.

I relaxed. "It's fine. What's going on?"

She explained that she'd just gotten back from the grocery store and had been carrying in groceries.

"Oh. How's the cabin?"

"It's cute," she said with a smile in her voice. "Very rustic. Vaulted, wooden ceilings. A fireplace. Decent sized kitchen with a patio, and grill. It looks smaller than the pictures, but I think you're going to love it. Oh… there's even a hot-tub."

"Yeah, that was one of the things that drew me in. Besides it being right on the lake. It's nice though, huh?"

"I love it. I think you will, too. Speaking of the lake, it's gorgeous, especially around sunset with all of the colorful leaves. I'm going to take a bunch of pictures tomorrow when you get here."

Brittany loved photography had an eye for capturing some pretty spectacular images. Every year she presented me with an album containing photos taken on our trips together.

"Oh, guess what?" she asked.

"What?"

"The manager hinted that some of the other tenants staying at the resort are involved with the film I told you about before."

"Really? That's cool."

It didn't surprise me. The place we'd booked at *Summit Lake Resort & Spa,* was brand new and offered both cabins and condos for rent. After having such a busy year, we'd splurged on a cabin, which was six-hundred a night. I knew some of the others were even bigger, and much more luxurious, which would obviously appeal to the celebrities and film crew.

"I can't wait to find out who's in it. I'm thinking of hanging out *Waverly's* tonight and seeing if anyone famous walks in."

"The bar?"

"Yeah. It's right off of the main lobby."

I didn't know how she did it, but Brittany was comfortable being alone in those types of settings. I, on the other hand, couldn't do it. I just felt too self-conscious. Not to mention, I didn't want anyone to approach me, thinking I was looking for company.

"That's right," I said, staring down at the chipped, red nail polish on my toes. They hadn't been recolored since dumping Jack. I made a mental note to fix them before turning in for the night.

"I'm only going to have one or two if I do." She let out a sigh. "I probably won't, though. I don't know."

"If you do, just be careful," I replied. Normally, I wouldn't think about it, but I couldn't get the dead woman out of my head. Yes, it had happened at a different town, but one never knew.

"Yes, Mother," she said dryly and then perked up. "Although, maybe I'll meet a hunky actor or director and let him accompany me back for a nightcap. What time did you say you'd be arriving tomorrow?"

I snorted. "Not until six, probably."

"Plenty of time to make him fall in love so he'll whisk me away to his mansion in Hollywood," she teased. "Or, hell, I'll settle for a quick, hot fling if it gets us on the movie set."

Britt was all talk. She'd never have a one-night stand, even with a rich celebrity. The woman was even less promiscuous than I was, and my college friends used to tease me about being a prude. I didn't consider myself uptight. Just careful. Of course, when it had come to Jack, I'd thrown caution to the wind by jumping into a work relationship, resulting from a late dinner and too many glasses of wine.

Lesson learned.

"By the way, I made reservations for us at *Montecristo's* for Tuesday night. It's that five-star restaurant right across from *Waverly's*. Expensive, but I figured you and I deserved to treat ourselves."

I'd seen the menu, and she was right about two things: It *was* expensive and we both worked too hard to feel guilty about one meal.

"Sounds great. I'm looking forward to it."

"I was just thinking—I haven't been to a nice restaurant since Dan and I broke up last year. Not to mention that the last time I went to a salon, or pampered myself, was around Valentine's Day." She let out a snort. "I have two cats, a bookcase overflowing with paperbacks I've already read, and a dusty makeup case. I'm not even thirty and Dad's life is more exciting than mine."

"I hear you," I replied, being in the same boat myself.

She went on. "I don't know. Maybe I should try one of those dating sites? Not that I need a man in my life, but I sure as hell miss date-nights and breakfast in bed."

"Why don't you try and cut back on some of your hours at work? So… you can get back into the social scene."

"Because the idea of a first date makes me quiver—and not in a good way. I just loathe the awkwardness of it all."

"I know what you mean. There's always Tinder, although I don't think you'd be picked up and pampered the way you'd like."

She sighed. "Tried it."

My eyes widened. "Really. You *did*?"

"Yes. I never told you, but it's how I met Dan. That's why I'll never use that app again."

I didn't know much about Dan, other than he'd started out sweet and had turned into a bossy, manipulative jerk. Thankfully, Brittany had ended it with him, although it hadn't been easy for her. She'd loved the guy and had almost taken him back, until I'd set her straight.

"I don't blame you."

"What about you? You ever try it?"

"Me?" I snorted. "No."

"Maybe we're destined to be single for the rest of our lives," she muttered. "On a good note, they say not having a guy in your life makes you live longer."

"Who said that?"

"I don't know. I saw an article on Facebook. Men can cause you more stress than children."

Considering what I'd gone through with Jack, I didn't exactly disagree. But, I also knew it was unfair to lump every man into that category. Plus, I'd met a lot of nutty females, working for a divorce lawyer. "I bet a woman wrote that article," I replied. I could have written it myself a short time ago. "Also, you can kick a man to the curb, but your kids are your kids. You're stuck with them. Now tell me that's not more stressful."

"I guess I'll never know. Apparently, children aren't in the stars for me. Remember when I went to that psychic and asked her how many children I'd have? You should have seen her face. She quickly changed the subject and never answered me. I'm not meant to have kids."

Personally, I didn't believe in psychics, horoscopes, or anything like that. Brittany was obsessed with all things supernatural, however. So was Dad.

"I wouldn't worry about it. If you can't have kids, for health reasons, I'll be a surrogate."

"Aww… I love you," she said with a smile in her voice.

"I love you, too. I know you'd do the same for me."

"Of course."

I yawned and stood up. "I should let you go. What are you doing for dinner tonight?"

"Crap, I almost forgot. After I unpack I'm supposed to be meeting Rocky and Jan at *Auntie K's Diner*. I'm going to be late if I don't get moving."

"Okay. Have fun. Say 'hello' to them for me."

"Will do."

"Wait, did you hear anything else about the dead woman found in Bear Creek?"

"I haven't had a chance to ask about it or watch the news. If I hear anything more, though, I'll tell you."

"Okay, thanks. See you soon."

"Definitely."

"Let me know if you run into anyone famous, too."

She chuckled. "I probably won't, but if I do get lucky, in more ways than one, you'll be the first to know."

"More like the third, right?"

"Yeah. Right," she said, sounding distracted. "Rocky's calling. I gotta go, I'll call you later. Bye."

"Bye."

Chapter 5

The Director

"WOULD YOU LIKE some more coffee?" asked Joanne, the tall, rail-thin waitress serving me at *Auntie K's*, a small diner in Summit Lake. A framed article by the front counter proclaimed it to be rated #9 for one of Minnesota's best kept secrets in the Midwest Food and Life Magazine two years ago. Although I'd only had the pie, I'd seen some of the food coming out of the kitchen, and it was definitely impressive. I made a mental note to come back for breakfast soon.

"No. I'm good," I told her, glancing at my watch. It was after nine already. I knew I'd been lingering in the restaurant for too long, but the raven-haired beauty two booths away was making it hard to leave. She was with an older couple, and from their conversation, I'd learned that she was from out of town. I guessed her to be somewhere in her mid-twenties and simply… stunning. With her long, graceful neck, high cheekbones, and light-green eyes, she reminded me a bit of the actress Charlize Theron, only with dark hair.

"You sure you don't want another piece of apple pie?" she asked.

I looked up and smiled politely. Joanne looked weary and I knew she was probably getting tired of refilling my coffee. "No, thank you. I'll just take the check."

She nodded. "Okay."

After paying for my meal, I walked out of the restaurant and noticed there were only a handful of vehicles in the parking lot besides mine. One of them, a red Jeep, had a Michigan license plate. I walked past it and got into my car. Instead of starting the engine, I sat in the darkness, wrestling with my impulses, which were pretty demanding at the moment. Right now, more than anything, I wanted the woman in the diner to star in my next film. Needed her to. Oh, she would make the perfect Marion.

On the other hand, it was one hell of a risk.

I wasn't wearing any kind of disguise. Not to mention that it was much too soon since Amber. I usually waited before hunting for a new victim.

At least a month.

Of course, I knew her ex-boyfriend would be number one on the list of suspects. Truthfully, I almost felt sorry for the big oaf. The autopsy scene had left her in pretty rough shape and I knew her family would be out for some blood of their own. Tommy would more than likely take the fall, and, hell, he was prison-bound anyway.

Those last moments, though.

Talk about gruesome.

At one point, I'd even needed a few shots of Cuervo to get through the scenes. In the end, however, the film had turned out excellent and I'd gotten top dollar for it. Thanks to Amber, who'd played her part well and had screamed her pretty little head off just at the right moments.

Smiling, I imagined the horror the two hikers must have felt after stumbling upon her. I would have loved to have gotten their reactions on film.

Closing my eyes, I raked my fingers through my hair. Common sense told me that taking another victim so soon was just asking for a shit storm. But I also knew that perfection sometimes came with a price and most things that mattered in life weren't easily obtained anyway. You had to work for them.

That's what Mother used to say. As terrible as she'd been, the bitch had given me some good life lessons.

I heard voices coming from outside. I opened my eyes and was pleased to see my lovely new obsession walking with the older couple toward the Jeep. She had on a red ski jacket and a red cap, almost reminding me of Little Red Riding Hood. I grinned.

The Big Bad Wolf has you in his sights...

She laughed at something the old man said and I was once again reminded of how beautiful she was by seeing her smile.

Oh, yes. Without a doubt. I knew that she would make the perfect Marion.

I began to envision it more and more. The only downfall was that I'd need to bleach her hair blonde, or find a wig. Other than that, the lead female role in *my* version of *Psycho* had this gorgeous girl's name written all over it.

There was more laughter and then threesome hugged each other goodbye and went their separate ways.

Making up my mind, I started my engine and followed her Jeep. Fifteen minutes later, she entered the *Summit Lake Resort & Spa* parking lot and I knew it had to be a sign.

Adrenaline pumping, I followed her slowly, hanging back as she drove past the hotel condos and toward the cabins. She eventually slowed to one of the smaller ones, opened the garage, and entered.

Feeling better than ever about my newest conquest, I continued past her place until I reached the end of the service road and then circled back. As I neared her cabin again, I expected the woman to be inside and was surprised to find her walking back toward the resort's entrance.

Curious as to whether she might be meeting someone in the hotel, or just taking a quick stroll, I drove past her and parked my car in the main lot, directly across from the lobby. I turned off my vehicle and sat quietly, waiting. After about a minute, she reached the lobby's entrance and went inside.

Dying to know what she was up to, I slipped out of my car and followed her into the building.

Although it was almost nine-thirty, the lobby was alive with guests checking in, which wasn't much of a surprise for a Saturday night. Hoping I wouldn't bump into anyone I knew, I quickly looked around but saw no sign of the woman.

Frowning, I walked over to the gift shop and peeked inside. Unfortunately, it was dead and I caught the attention of the cashier, Trina, who recognized me.

"Oh, hey," she said, looking up from the magazine she was reading. "How's it going?"

"Good," I replied. "Have a good night."

Normally, I stuck around and chatted longer and I could tell from Trina's expression that she was disappointed. "You, too."

I turned and headed over to the entrance of *Waverly's*. When I stepped inside, I found my beauty right away. She was sitting at the bar, ordering a drink. Our eyes met for a brief second and then she looked away.

Knowing that I couldn't be seen around her if this was really going to happen, I turned around and walked out of the restaurant.

THIRTY MINUTES LATER, I had on a black ski mask and was inside her bedroom, with a flashlight and my tool bag. As luck would have it, she'd left her patio door unlocked and I'd managed to sneak in easily. Another sign that this was meant to be.

Feeling confident, I walked over to the bed where she'd set a large, blue spinner suitcase. I unzipped it and went through her things, needing to get a sense of who she was. Interestingly enough, I didn't find anything sexy in her articles of clothing. Everything was made of cotton, polyester, and wool. As beautiful as she was, her wardrobe was rather dull and boring.

A noise in the other room caught my ear. Realizing that she must have returned already, I raced over to the closet and hid inside, my heart pounding.

A few seconds later, a song by Lady Gaga filled the cabin.

Bad Romance.

She began singing along to the lyrics, loud enough that I could hear her all the way into the bedroom. Listening to her belt out the words with such emotion made me smile.

Her screams were going to shake the foundation.

I just knew it.

As her voice grew nearer, I realized in dismay that I'd left my bag of tools on the bed. Unfortunately, there was no time to retrieve it, because the light switched on in the bedroom.

Dammit.

I watched through the vents in the panel door as she approached the bed and stopped singing.

"What the hell?" she said, staring down at the bag.

Knowing that her confusion would soon turn to terror, I became giddy with excitement.

She reached for the bag and unzipped it while I quietly slipped out of the closet. Sensing my presence, she whirled around.

I grinned at her. "Sorry. That's mine."

Taking in my dark clothes, mask, and gloves, she cried out and then turned to flee.

I lunged forward and grabbed her around the waist. Before she could make any more noise, I covered her mouth with my hand.

53

"Save your voice for later," I said, pulling her back against my chest while she kicked and flailed. "When it counts."

She bit my gloved hand.

I roared in pain and almost released her, but somehow managed to keep my hold.

"You *bitch*," I growled, resisting the urge to snap her neck.

She fought me all the way over to the bed. I pushed her down, rolled her over, and straddled her.

"Please, let me go!"

"Calm down and you won't get hurt," I said through clenched teeth.

Ignoring me, the woman began beating my chest.

I reached for the tool bag and quickly grabbed my switchblade. "Enough!" I growled, flicking it open and bringing it to her throat.

Her eyes filled with terror. "Please," she begged. "Don't."

"What's your name?"

"Bri... Brittany." She closed her eyes and began to sob.

"Calm down, Brittany."

She opened her eyes again. "What do you want?" she asked, trembling.

She thought I wanted to rape her. I could see it in her eyes. I smirked. "Not what you might think."

"I have money," she said quickly. "I put most of it in the safe. The combination is 4444. Please, take it. I won't even report you."

"I'm not here for that, either, although one could always use a few extra bucks." I reached inside of the tool bag and pulled out a roll of duct tape.

She swallowed. "What do you want then?"

"An actress."

She looked confused. "What? I'm not an actress."

"Yes. You are," I said, before ripping off a piece of duct tape with my teeth. "And let me tell you, you just *aced* the audition."

Brittany's face turned white.

I placed the tape over her mouth. "Tell me, Brittany, have you ever seen the movie *Psycho*?"

She shook her head.

"Really? It was my mother's favorite," I said, my voice trailing off as I remembered how we'd watch it over and over again. "My version is going to be so much better, though." I grinned. "Pardon me, *our* version."

Tears spilled out of Brittany's eyes and her body shook as she sobbed.

I caressed the side of her cheek. She smelled lovely. Almost like vanilla. Soon, she would smell like Chanel and grace the camera with her beauty and ear-piercing screams. "Hush, now, beautiful. Save your cries for later."

AFTER INJECTING BRITTANY with a heavy sedative, I waited for her to fall asleep and then grabbed the keys to her SUV. I picked her up and carried her to the Jeep, put her in the back, returned to the house, and located the small safe. The numbers she gave me worked and I was pleasantly surprised to find ten one-hundred dollar bills tucked inside. I closed the safe, put the money into my wallet, and checked the cabin once more, making sure I hadn't left anything incriminating behind. A short time later, we were on the road and heading toward Bear Creek.

Although it was probably too early for anyone to notice Brittany was missing, it wasn't until we reached the farmhouse that I began to relax. I parked the Jeep in front of the garage and sat there for a moment, the tension slowly ebbing away. It was hard to believe that everything had went as smoothly as it had. As far as I could tell, I was in the clear and felt a great sense of accomplishment.

Content, I looked at the tall, debilitated house, which had been built in 1876. Even at night it was an eyesore and appeared as tired as the surrounding landscape. The white paint was weathered and peeling. The wood underneath was obviously warped and cracked. The slanted roof leaked and needed to be replaced. Not to mention that the porch sagged like an old woman's bosom. The inside wasn't much better. Most of the furniture was from the seventies, including the large console television set and gaudy flower-patterned sofa and loveseat. The living room was sunken and wasn't supposed to be. The staircase leading up to the four bedrooms upstairs was dangerously creaky. Not to mention there was a musty smell that permeated throughout the house. But, it captured the kind of creepy atmosphere I needed for my movies. Also, the rent was so cheap that I'd ended up paying out of pocket for the entire year, although I would be moving on soon.

I heard Brittany moaning in her sleep and decided it was time to bring her inside. Unfortunately, it had been long day and carrying her up the stairs proved to be a pain. But, I managed without dropping her.

Once we were in the bedroom, I chained her to the bed, gave her another shot of the sedative, and locked her inside before slipping away until morning.

Chapter 6

Whitney

I ACTUALLY SLEPT well, until a nightmare jolted me awake. I opened my eyes and sat up in bed, my heart still racing from the horrible images. Brittany and I'd been chased by a creature with round button-eyes and a red sewn-in mouth. Its head had been made out of burlap. The hair out of thick, black yarn. It was terrifying and reminded me of a giant voodoo doll. The damn thing had seemed so real, too, especially when the monster grabbed my sister and began running off with her. The terror I felt is what actually woke me.

Sighing, I curled back under the covers and blamed the nightmare on the dark chocolate I'd eaten before bedtime. Brittany had claimed that sweets gave people nightmares. I had no idea if it was a scientific fact, but was now a believer.

Closing my eyes, I suddenly remembered that she'd been thinking about going to *Waverly's* after dinner with Rocky and Jan. It made me wonder if she'd met anyone.

I glanced at the clock and saw it was only three-thirty in the morning. Too early to call and check on her.

I thought about the victim in Bear Creek.

Maybe I should just send her a text?

Telling myself that I was being paranoid, I adjusted my pillow, closed my eyes, and eventually fell back asleep.

When my alarm sounded at five a.m., I wanted nothing more than to go back to sleep, but remembered the long drive ahead of me.

Yawning, I got up, took a shower, loaded my luggage into the back of my LaCrosse, and took one last look around the condo. Satisfied that I hadn't forgotten anything, I locked everything up and drove to a nearby coffee shop, where I ordered a caramel frappe and a bagel to go.

As I headed out of town, it started to rain. I turned on my windshield wipers, along with the radio.

I hadn't checked the weather report, so wasn't sure what I'd be driving through. I also didn't particularly care. It had been months since I'd had an entire week off and I was determined that nothing was going to ruin my good mood. Even shitty weather.

I WAITED UNTIL nine to call my sister and left her a message when she didn't answer. It wasn't a big surprise, considering that Britt was a night-owl and used to working third shifts at the hospital.

As I was hanging up, I remembered my promise to call our father and dialed him. As luck would have it, he didn't answer either. Part of me was relieved. I wasn't in the mood to talk and our conversations usually ended up in arguments. At least the recent ones.

"Hey, Dad. It's me, Whitney. Just calling to see how you've been. I'm on my way up to Summit Lake. You've probably already heard that Britt and I are renting a cabin for a week, near Rocky and Jan's place. Anyway, I was told that you and…" I forced her name from my lips, "Lillian are in the French Riviera. Sounds exotic and…" I wanted to say expensive but didn't, "ah… fun. Anyway, I hope you're enjoying yourself. Stay safe. Love you. Bye."

I hung up and was about eat the rest of my bagel when the phone rang. Thinking it was Dad, or Britt, I was surprised to find Uncle Rocky on the other end.

"Hi, kiddo. You on your way up?" he asked with a grin in his voice.

"As a matter of fact, I am. How are things going up there?" I replied, smiling. "It's been awhile since we've talked."

"Pretty good and yeah. It has. We need to keep in better contact."

"I know. It's my fault. I've been so busy with work. That's going to change soon."

"Oh, really? Are you getting a new job?"

"Possibly," I said, thinking of Jack. Probably, was more like it. "Anyway, how was dinner last night? I heard you were meeting up with Britt."

He told me they'd had a nice evening. "We're looking forward to seeing you as well."

"I miss you guys, too. How's Jan?"

"She's doing well. Better than last week."

"What do you mean?"

He explained that she'd been convinced she'd had a kidney infection and had gone to the E.R. Fortunately, Jan had only strained a muscle in her lower back.

"How'd she do that?"

"I don't know. The doctor said she needed to get off the sofa more and exercise. He thinks that's why her back may have went out."

"Jan? She's the last person I'd suspect of being a couch potato," I mused. If anything, the woman never sat down and was always busy cleaning or working in her garden.

"Well, she hurt her toe a few weeks back. Wacked it against the coffee table when she was vacuuming. Good, grief, the cuss words that came from that woman's mouth…," he said with a smile in his voice. "Anyway, because of that, she'd been taking it easy. Ever since the doctor told her she needed to get off of her duff, Jan has been a little dynamo. She's even started jogging and has been nagging me about doing it, too."

"You haven't yet?"

"No. I keep myself busy enough. Hell, I'm going to be sixty-five soon. Jogging might put me into an early grave. Especially with these bad knees of mine."

"I didn't know you had bad knees."

"They're old knees. As far as I'm concerned that means they're bad. Plus, being six-foot-one doesn't help. I bet you didn't know that I used to be six-three," he said. "That tells you something right there."

I didn't know if he was joking or serious. One thing about Rocky was that you could never tell. He also liked to gripe a lot. As did Dad.

We talked a little more and then I asked him about the murder in Bear Creek.

"The woman's name was Amber," he said grimly. "The authorities believe that her boyfriend probably did it. Apparently, he's known around town as a hot head. Not to mention that the two had gotten into a pretty heated argument before she disappeared. Sheriff Baldwin said it was a pretty gruesome crime scene though. The maniac did a number on the poor young woman."

I cringed. "Really?"

"Yeah. Apparently guys were losing their lunches. They never saw anything like it. A lot of blood and missing skin. She was pretty mutilated. The poor thing."

I shuddered. It was more than I'd needed to know. "Did they arrest the boyfriend?"

"Yeah, he's in jail right now. Apparently, this isn't the first time he's been arrested. Last year they got him for aggravated assault, although the charges were later dropped."

"Huh."

"I don't think he's going to get so lucky this time," he said wryly.

Imagining what kind of sick, twisted person it took to mutilate another, I certainly hoped not.

"Anyway, Jan and I are heading out to the grocery store. I just wanted to call and make sure you're doing well and let you know that we're excited to see you."

"Same here, Uncle Rocky. I'll see you soon."

"Sounds good. Drive safely."

Chapter 7

The Director

"I KNOW YOU'RE awake," I said to Brittany after entering the bedroom.

She turned her head to face me and just like before, I had on the black ski mask to hide my identity.

I leaned down and pulled the duct tape off her mouth. Her cheeks were stained with mascara and her eyes were red-rimmed from crying. It would have been a great scene for a movie, but not the one I was doing with her.

A shame.

Brittany took a couple of deep breaths and then began to cry again. "Please... take these shackles off. My wrists and ankles are killing me."

I knew she wasn't lying. I'd had no choice but to keep her restrained while I was away. Unfortunately, I'd been gone longer than planned and felt a small stab of guilt. Especially when my eyes trailed down from her wrists to her jeans, where there was a dark stain in the crotch.

She'd urinated on herself.

Of course, I'd expected it, which is why I'd put plastic under her. Under all of them. One never knew when things were going to get messy.

"We need to clean you up. Also, I brought you some food," I said, holding up the white bag in my hand. "I'm sure you're hungry. There's a turkey and bacon club in here with your name on it."

"Thank you," she croaked, staring up at me fearfully.

Manners.

That was good.

She was either deciding to play nice for survival or biding herself some time while coming up with an escape plan. We would soon see.

"You're welcome."

She licked her lips, which I noticed were already dry and cracked from dehydration. "Do you have any water?"

I pulled out a bottle from the bag and unscrewed the cap. "Sorry it took me so long to get back here," I said, leaning down to hold her head up. I brought the bottle to her lips.

She drank too fast and began to choke.

"Careful." I patted her on the back gently until she stopped coughing. "You okay?"

Brittany nodded.

I stood up and screwed the cap back onto the bottle. "Not to be rude, but you're smelling pretty ripe. Let's get you into the shower and then you can eat the sandwich." I put the bottle on the nightstand.

Brittany's eyes widened in fear.

"Don't worry. I'm not going to hold your hand while you're in there. In fact, you can have the bathroom all to yourself."

She relaxed.

I looked at her long, dark brown hair and asked her how she felt about changing it.

Brittany gave me a strange look.

"Your character is blonde." I touched her hair and she shrank away from me in fear. I pulled my hand away. "I thought about buying you a wig, but people in small towns tend to gossip. So, I've decided to bleach your hair instead. I've ordered a couple of kits online. They're supposed to arrive here by tomorrow."

"Please, let me go," she begged, her eyes searching mine. "I'll forget this ever happened. I won't even go to the police. I promise."

I knew she wasn't going to shut up about being set free. None of them did. So, I told her what she wanted to hear. What they *all* wanted to hear. I lied. "I'll let you go."

Her eyes narrowed slightly. "You will?"

I nodded. "Yes. But, only after we've finished."

"Making the movie?"

I nodded.

She still didn't look too convinced.

AFTER REMOVING THE shackles, I pulled a gun out of my leather jacket and warned her to behave.

"I will," Brittany replied, staring at the gun.

"Good." I took a step back from the bed. "Okay. Let's get you cleaned up."

She slowly got up out of the bed.

"The bathroom is down the hallway. You'll find soap and shampoo inside."

"What am I supposed to wear?" she asked, rubbing her wrists.

"There's a robe I left for you inside. It's hanging on the hook."

Brittany stood there silently with a pensive look on her face.

I waved the gun toward the doorway. "Let's go."

She walked out of the bedroom and I followed.

"The bathroom is to the right," I said as we headed down the hallway.

Brittany found it and stepped inside. She turned around and looked at me. I knew what she was wondering from the expression in her eyes.

"Don't worry. Like I said before, you can have your privacy. I'll wait out here."

Looking relieved, she shut and locked the door.

Sighing, I leaned back against the wall across from the bathroom and pictured her looking out the window, wondering if she could possibly escape. Even if she made it out and managed to climb down to the lower part of the roof, it would still be a twelve-foot drop. There was no way that she could make it without breaking any bones. I just hoped that she wasn't stupid enough to try it. I'd have to kill her and find a new Marion.

WHEN SHE WAS finished in the bathroom, Brittany opened up the door. Her face was now void of all makeup. She looked and smelled fresh.

My eyes dipped to the robe. "How do you like it?"

"Like what?"

"The robe."

She looked down at it and shrugged.

"It's not an exact match to the one Janet Leigh wore in Psycho, but it's similar. This one is pink. I think the original was blue."

She stared at me in disbelief. "You really want me to help you re-enact the movie *Psycho*? That's really the only reason why you kidnapped me?"

"Yes. The movie is very important to me."

Brittany frowned. "And if I do this, you'll really let me go?"

"You'll be as free as a bird," I said, waving my arms and smiling.

She wasn't amused. "Okay. When do we get started on the film?"

"We have a few things to do, first. Besides lightening your hair, we need to make sure it's the same length as Janet's was," I said, reaching over to touch it.

She pulled away. "You're going to cut it?"

"I'm afraid so. Don't worry. It will look beautiful," I reassured her.

Brittany stared at for me a minute and nodded reluctantly. "Okay. Fine."

I grinned. "Good."

Her eyes went back to the gun I was holding. "You're not going to harm me during the scene, are you?"

The sadist in me ached to tell her the truth and see her face light up with terror. But, I needed to save all of her true horror for the camera. Not to mention that I needed her to sit still while I cut and lightened her hair. Her compliance would make everything so much easier.

"No, of course not," I lied.

She stared at me hard, trying to gauge if I was really telling her the truth. "So, this is really just about making a movie?"

She was having such a tough time wrapping her mind around this. I couldn't blame her. Still, the questions were getting on my nerves. Even I was getting sick of lying. "Yes. A reenactment of one of the most famous horror movies of all time."

"But, why?"

"Because, I want to prove that I can do it better. In memory of my mother."

"Is she alive?"

"She died a few years ago."

"Oh." Brittany's eyes searched mine, still looking for the truth. "Why can't you just hire actresses to do this? Why kidnap them?"

"To save money," I replied. "Beautiful women do not come without a price."

She began asking more questions and I cut her off.

"The less you know about me, the better," I said firmly. "No more questions."

"Okay. She sighed.

"You should eat that sandwich I brought for you."

Nodding, she headed back to the bedroom with me at her heels. Once inside, I told her to remove the plastic sheet from the bed and put it into the corner of the room.

"I'm sorry for the accident," she said, looking embarrassed as she did the chore.

I hid my smile. I'd filmed several women for my movies. Either they'd fought tooth-and-nail to try and escape, or they tried befriending me. It was a relief that Brittany was trying to get through this rationally. I wasn't in the fighting mood.

"It's okay."

After Brittany was finished, I handed her the bag of food and she sat down on the mattress. She pulled the sandwich out of the bag. "Can I call my sister and let her know that I'm all right?"

I smirked. "You know I can't let you do that."

"She'll be worried and go to the police. They'll search everywhere for me. Probably here, too. I mean, this town isn't *that* big."

"You think we're in Summit Lake still," I said, amused.

"We're not?" She frowned. "Where are we?"

I winked. "We're at the Bates Motel, remember?"

Brittany stared at me in confusion.

"Don't worry about it. Just, eat your food," I said, nodding toward her sandwich.

While unwrapping the sandwich, she asked about her Jeep.

"I had to dispose of it," I replied.

It had been a pain in the ass, too. After driving it to the next town over, I parked it deep in the woods and then walked three miles to a gas station. From there, I called an Uber to take me back to my own vehicle.

She started asking me more questions and I cut her off.

"The less you know, the better," I reminded. "Unless, you don't want to be set free later."

Her eyes flashed with panic. "I do. Sorry, I won't ask you anything else."

If I had a dime for every time a captive said that to me…

"All you have to know is that if you play nice, you won't get hurt. Okay?"

She nodded.

It was such a cliché line, but it always shut them up. At least for a few hours.

Chapter 8

Whitney

I TRIED PHONING Brittany several times, but still there wasn't an answer, so I left her another voicemail. I was beginning to feel like she was avoiding me.

"It's me again. Just calling to see how you're doing. You're starting to worry me, Britt." I sighed. "Anyway, I should be there in another two hours or so. Call me back, please."

After hanging up, I dialed Rocky and told him that I still hadn't heard from Britt.

"This isn't like her. She should have called me back a long time ago," I told him. "I'm concerned. Have you heard from her at all?"

"No," he replied, surprised. "I haven't spoken to her all day. Should I take a ride over to the resort and check on her?"

"If you don't mind."

"Not at all."

I sighed in relief. "Thank you."

"Of course. I want to make sure she's safe, too. How are the roads, by the way? We're getting a lot of rain here."

"It's pretty stormy," I said as a flash of lightning lit up the sky above me.

"Take your time and get here safely. Let us worry about Brittany. Okay?"

"Sure. Call me as soon as you find out anything."

"Will do."

TWENTY MINUTES LATER, Rocky called me back.

"I'm here at the cabin and she's not answering the door," he said, sounding concerned. "I'm going to see if the staff at the resort will let me in."

My stomach tightened in fear. "Is her Jeep there?"

"There's a garage. I can't tell if it's parked inside or not."

"She was going to have a nightcap at the bar last night," I said, trying not to panic.

"What bar?"

"The one in the lobby. *Waverly's*. What if she brought someone home and... oh, God. Please let her be okay."

"Would she bring someone back?" he asked, surprised.

"I don't think so. Britt isn't like that. But, it doesn't mean that someone didn't follow her."

"Oh, hell. Now you have *me* scared half to death," he muttered. "I'll go and talk to the staff and make them let me in or else."

"Okay. Keep me posted."

He promised he would and then we both hung up.

IT TOOK ROCKY thirty agonizing minutes before he finally got back to me.

"The manager let me in. Fortunately, we know each other or I don't think he would have," Rocky said. "Anyway, her Jeep is gone and she's nowhere to be found. Maybe she's grocery shopping?"

"She told me she did that yesterday," I replied, a little relieved. At least he hadn't walked into something horrifying.

"Good grief, I hope nothing bad has happened to her," he mumbled.

I was about to ask him to see if it looked like she'd used the shower when he began talking to someone with him.

"Uh, oh," he said.

"What is it?"

"Her purse is here with her I.D. and wallet." He sighed. "As well as her cell phone. That explains why she isn't calling you back."

Tears filled my eyes. This was bad. I just knew it. "She wouldn't ever leave without her phone or wallet."

"I'm going to take a drive into town and see if her Jeep is around. I'm also going to put in a call to Sheriff Baldwin. Hopefully, she just forgot her purse and there's nothing serious going on."

As much as I wanted to believe that, in my heart of hearts, I felt nothing but dread.

Chapter 9

Whitney

IT WAS JUST after six when I finally arrived in Summit Lake. I called Rocky as soon as I passed the green *Welcome* sign.

"I'm here," I said to his voicemail when he didn't answer. "Call me back so I know what's happening and where to go."

After hanging up, I drove to the center of town first and began searching for my sister's Jeep. As I was nearing the library, my phone rang. It was Rocky.

"Where are you?" he asked.

"I'm downtown, by the library. Any news yet?"

"No," he said in a grim voice. "I'm with Sheriff Baldwin right now. Why don't you stop over at the police station and meet us here."

A lump formed in my throat. *Where in the hell was she?* "Okay."

AFTER LOCATING THE station, I hurried through the rain and entered the building. Wiping my cheeks dry, I headed over to an attendant, who directed me to Sheriff Baldwin's office. When I arrived, Rocky, who Brittany and I both agreed looked a little like Harrison Ford, was seated on the other side of his desk and both men were in deep conversation.

I cleared my throat. "Hello."

The two turned my way and then Rocky stood up. He walked over and gave me a hug.

"It's so good to see you," he said, patting me gently on the back.

"You, too. So... nothing yet I take it?" I asked, suddenly feeling overwhelmed. Knowing that the police were now involved made this even more serious.

"Unfortunately, no." He turned to the other man. "Sheriff, this is my niece, Whitney. Britt's twin."

Sheriff Baldwin, a heavy-set man with short white hair and kind blue eyes, reached over and shook my hand. "Nice to meet you. How's the weather out there? Still raining?"

"Pretty much," I replied. "Sorry, I'm getting everything wet. I didn't have an umbrella."

"Eh, don't worry about it. Hopefully, it will let up soon. It's definitely not making things easier for us. Please," he motioned to the other open chair, next to Rocky. "Make yourself comfortable."

"Thank you." I sat down. "So… what are we doing about Brittany?" I asked, unzipping my wet parka.

"I've already put out an alert, so hopefully we'll hear something soon. Do you have any recent pictures of her?" the sheriff asked.

"I have some from a couple of months ago," I replied, pulling my phone out. "I can send them to you."

The sheriff looked please. "That would be great."

"Otherwise, they're identical twins," Rocky said. "You could probably just take a photo of Whitney and use that."

"She keeps her hair longer," I reminded him, touching my own hair. It was down to my shoulders, whereas Britt usually wore hers down to the middle of her back.

Rocky nodded. "True. Also, now that I think about it, her hair is quite a bit darker."

"I had mine lightened last month," I explained. It was now almost a honey-blonde color. I'd done it after Jack had mentioned he thought the color would

79

look good on me. I thought it was fine, but preferred it darker.

"It looks nice," Rocky said, looking sad.

"Thank you."

"So, we should definitely use an actual photo of your sister," the sheriff said.

I nodded and began scrolling through my pictures. I found one I'd taken of the two of us. It was from the end beginning of August, the last time we'd actually gotten together. We'd been at a hole-in-the-wall near her condo, called *Don's Bar and Grille*. They served awesome burgers and I had her take me there every time I visited. Seeing the two of us together, so happy, brought tears to my eyes. The thought of Britt being hurt, or worse, was almost too inconceivable to imagine.

Noticing that I was getting emotional, Rocky put his arm around my shoulders. "We'll find her," he said softly.

I nodded and scrolled further back until I found one of Britt alone. She was sitting in her Jeep and smiling at a joke I'd made before snapping the picture. Once again, she looked so carefree and happy. "Will this work?" I asked Sheriff Baldwin, holding my phone toward him.

"Yes," he replied.

"Where should I send it?"

He gave me an email address.

"Have you spoken to your dad about her being missing?" Rocky asked.

"No. I left him a message earlier. It wasn't about Brittany, though," I said, feeling guilty about not calling him back. I'd totally blocked him out.

Rocky took out his phone. "He needs to know. I'll call him."

"I haven't seen Rollin in years. Where is he? In Michigan?" the sheriff asked.

"Normally. He's vacationing right now in the French Riviera," I said.

Rocky snorted. "Well, la dee da. Let me guess, it has something to do with that high school student he's dating?"

"What was that?" Sheriff Baldwin asked, staring at Rocky in horror.

"Relax, I'm just kidding. My brother *is* dating someone young enough to be his daughter, though," he said. "She's in her twenties."

"Twenties, huh? Well more power to him," Sheriff Baldwin said before returning to his laptop.

I rolled my eyes. As far as I was concerned, dating a woman that much younger, especially one who had nothing in common with Dad, was sickening. I imagined that if *I* were dating someone in their sixties, my father wouldn't exactly approve, either.

"You don't like her, do you?" Rocky asked, staring at me after dialing the number.

"Do you?" I volleyed.

"I like her if she makes him happy. After your mom died—hey, Rollin, it's me. Rocky," he said into the phone.

I listened as he explained what was happening.

"She doesn't have her phone," Rocky said, looking at me as he spoke. "We found her purse in the cabin."

They spoke for a few more seconds and then Rocky handed me the phone. "He wants to talk to you."

I took it from him. "Hi."

"I can't believe this is happening," he said, all choked up. "What are your thoughts in all of this? Do you think she might be with someone she knows and just forgot her purse and phone?"

"I want to believe that, but I don't," I replied. "I think she's in trouble."

He let out a moan and then I heard Lillian's voice in the background.

"They're calling about Britt. She's disappeared. We have to get back to Minnesota," Dad said to her.

She made a reply, but I couldn't understand it.

"No, I don't think she's just being irresponsible," he said, sounding irritated. "She's not like that. Neither of my daughters are."

"Dad, are you coming out here then?" I interrupted, wanting to get off the phone before I blasted Lillian.

"Yes. We'll be flying out as soon as we can."

"Okay. Call me when you arrive and we'll come and get you."

"Thanks, sweetie. If you get in touch with her, let me know."

"Will do."

"I'll see you soon. Love you."

"Love you, too," I replied.

I hung up and then the three of us decided to drive over to the cabin. I followed Rocky and Sheriff Baldwin in my car, all the while praying I'd see Brittany's Jeep parked somewhere. But there was no sign of her and as the clocked ticked, I knew that this *definitely* wasn't just her being careless. Something was dreadfully wrong.

When we arrived at the resort we stopped in at the main lobby first and spoke to Sheila, the manager on duty.

Sheila, a tall, heavy-set woman with dark hair and warm brown eyes, gave us a horrified look. "Oh no. I heard about that. She's still missing?"

"Yes, unfortunately," Sheriff Baldwin said. He handed her the photo he'd printed out of my sister. "This is Brittany Halverson. She's twenty-seven and staying in cabin number 8. She checked in yesterday and we believe that she may have stopped in at *Waverly's* last night, for a drink."

Sheila studied the photo. "I wasn't working yesterday, so I didn't see her in the lobby. Pretty girl."

"Yes, she is," Rocky murmured.

"Would you mind if we questioned some of your staff? To see if anyone may have seen her last night or even today?" Sheriff Baldwin asked.

"I'll do you one better," Sheila said, handing him back the photo. "I'll check the camera footage and help you ask around. Do you know what time she may have visited *Waverly's* last night?"

"She was with my wife and me until about nine o'clock. We were at *Aunty K's Diner* before she returned here," Rocky said. "So, I'm not entirely sure."

"Well, at least it's a good start," Sheila said, walking around the counter. "Let's go and talk to Ryan, one of the bartenders. I believe he was working last night."

"Sounds good," the sheriff said. "By the way, I hear you guys are busy with the movie crew staying here."

"Yes, we're fully booked," she replied as we followed her to the bar. She lowered her voice. "Two of our luxury cabins are being rented by celebrities."

"Oh, yeah? Who might those be?" Rocky asked.

"Marlow Frost and Jimmy Frank," she said. "But, you didn't hear that from me."

"I don't recognize either of their names. Of course, I don't watch many movies," Rocky replied. "What about you, Whitney? They ring a bell?"

"Yes. I've heard of them," I replied and told them what I knew. Marlow Frost was in her forties and usually starred in romantic comedies. Jimmy Frank was somewhere in his thirties and best known for his starring role in a popular macabre television series about circus oddities.

"Wait a second, isn't he the ringmaster in *The Travelers*?" Sheriff Baldwin asked.

"Yes," I replied, picturing the actor dressed in his costume. His character was supposed to secretly be Satan, enticing people into joining the circus and doing his dirty work.

"That's a pretty creepy show. I saw an episode once and had to switch it off halfway through," he said with a look of distaste. "Talk about morbid. I swear, the things people watch these days are unbelievable. No wonder there is so much violence in the world."

"I couldn't agree more," Sheila said. "It's a pretty dark series. That aside, Jimmy Frank is a pretty nice guy, even as famous as he is."

When we entered *Waverly's*, it was busy. There were two bartenders working, as well as a waitress,

85

and all three were racing around trying to serve everyone.

"Is it always like this?" Rocky asked.

"It's Happy Hour and there's a hockey game on," Sheila said. "Plus, the resort is fully booked, like I mentioned before."

We walked over to the bar and Sheila motioned for one of the bartenders to join us, a tall, bald man I'd guess to be in his fifties.

"Be there in a sec," he called out.

"So, that's Ryan?" the sheriff asked.

"Yes," Sheila replied, sitting down on the stool.

"Was anyone else working here last night on duty right now?" he asked, taking out his notepad.

"I don't know. I was off yesterday. I'm sure Ryan can tell us," she replied.

After pouring a pitcher of beer, Ryan wiped his hands on his apron and rushed over.

"What's up?" he asked with a curious look.

"Do you remember seeing this young woman in the bar last night? Sometime after nine?" Sheriff Baldwin asked, holding the photo up.

He looked at it and nodded right away. "She came in alone and didn't stay too long. Why?"

"She's missing," the sheriff replied, studying his face closely.

Ryan's eyes widened in surprise. "Really? Wow, sorry to hear that."

"If you don't mind, I'd like to interview you in a more private setting," he replied.

"You don't think I'm a suspect?" he asked, looking horrified.

"We're not even sure about foul play at this point," the sheriff replied. "So, relax, son."

Looking embarrassed, he smiled weakly. "Yeah, sure. It's hectic in here, though. Could you give me a few minutes first?"

"If you'd like, Ryan. I can take over. I used to bartend," Sheila said.

"Okay. That'll work for me, I guess," he replied, scratching his elbow.

"Do you have a quiet place for us to do the interview?" Sheriff Baldwin asked Sheila, just as a group of guys began to cheer at a hockey goal.

"Yeah, the North Banquet Room should be available," Sheila said. "Feel free to use it. I believe it's unlocked."

"Much obliged," Sheriff Baldwin replied. "Also, could you get me a list of everyone who was on staff at the resort last night? Their last names and phone numbers as well?"

"Do you really think that's necessary? I mean, she's just missing, right?" Sheila replied. "Shouldn't we wait?"

"Wait for what?" I asked, the pressure from all of this getting to me. I knew we had to move quickly. "For her to turn up dead?"

Sheila's face turned white. "No, I'm sorry. I didn't mean it to come out like that or to upset you."

She was obviously being sincere and I was taking my frustration out on her. "It's okay," I replied, softening. "I'm just so worried. This disappearing act is *not* like Brittany at all."

"Still, it was insensitive of me," she said. "Anyway, I'd better help Shawn serve these guys before they start complaining. Good luck finding her. And, Sheriff, I'll get you that list as soon as I can."

"Appreciate it," he replied and looked at the three of us. "Shall we?"

We followed Ryan out of the bar, through the hotel lobby, and then down a long hallway. As we neared one of restroom signs, Rocky excused himself.

"You guys go on. I'll find you. Jan has me drinking two liters of water a day," he said with a grim smile. "And nature is screaming my name loud and clear right now."

"Look for the North Banquet Room," reminded Sheriff Baldwin with a smirk.

"Will do," he replied.

A minute later, Ryan, the sheriff, and I were seated at one of the dining tables inside of the room, which was decorated for Halloween.

"Looks like the hotel is hosting some kind of Halloween party," remarked the Sheriff.

"Yeah," Ryan said. "One of the local businesses rented it out for their annual fundraiser. I'm not sure who."

Sheriff Baldwin looked over at an oversized spider in the corner and chuckled. "Looks like it will be a fun time. Well, good for them."

Ryan nodded and looked across the table at me. " So, are you the missing woman's twin?"

I nodded.

"I imagine you two are very close?" he asked.

I nodded.

"I'm also a twin. My brother died, many years ago, though," he replied, staring off.

"Sorry for your loss," I said softly. From the look on his face, he was still dealing with his brother's death. I wanted to ask Ryan what had happened, but stopped myself. It was probably a difficult subject.

"Thank you," he replied.

Sheriff Baldwin looked at me. "Normally, I'd conduct these interviews alone, but Ryan, here, might remember something that you could give us input on."

"Yeah, definitely," I replied, relieved I was allowed to sit in.

"So, Ryan, tell us what you saw last night," Sheriff Baldwin said, opening up a small notepad.

The bartender repeated what he'd told us earlier.

"So, she definitely came in alone?" the sheriff said, studying him intently.

Ryan adjusted the black leather rope bracelet he had on his wrist. "Yes. She sat down at the bar and ordered a glass of Lambrusco wine."

"Did anyone approach her?" the sheriff asked.

He scratched his temple and then nodded. "Actually, someone walked up to the bar and ordered a beer. While I was pouring it, he made a little conversation with her."

"Did he hit on her?" Sheriff Baldwin asked.

Ryan shook his head. "No. I think he may have asked what she was drinking. That's about it."

"Do you know who this guy is?" the sheriff asked.

"Just someone staying at the hotel," he replied. "He's getting to be a regular, though. I think he's part of the movie crew."

"Could you give me a name and description of him?" the sheriff asked as Rocky stepped into the banquet room.

"I believe his name is Charlie. I don't recall his last name, but I'm sure we could check the records from yesterday. He usually charges his items to his room."

"Good to know. Was Charlie alone?" the sheriff asked, as Rocky sat down next to me.

"No. He was with a couple other guys."

"Did anyone else approach Brittany or seem interested in her?" he asked. "You know, anyone *eyeballing* her?"

"I don't know, honestly. It didn't seem like anyone was obsessed with her, if that's what you're getting at."

As the questions continued, it was obvious that if someone had been taking special interest in my sister, Ryan didn't have a clue.

"So, she left alone?" the sheriff asked.

"Yes. And I watched her leave. From where I was standing, I didn't see anyone follow her out," he added with a grim expression.

"Do you know what time it was?" Sheriff Baldwin asked.

"It was between ten-fifteen and ten-thirty, I believe," he replied. "Somewhere in there."

"Did anyone leave shortly after Brittany?" the sheriff asked, absently clicking his pen several times.

"Now that, I couldn't tell you," he said. "I only noticed her leave because she'd been at the bar. Sorry."

"The cameras in the bar will show us if anyone else left after her," Rocky piped in.

"True." The sheriff looked at me. "Do you have any questions for him?"

"Actually, I do." I looked at Ryan. "What was Brittany doing when she was sitting down, by herself?"

He shrugged and then something came to him. "Actually, I remember that she was on her phone quite a bit. I feel like she may have been texting someone."

"Did she look upset at all while she was doing this?" the sheriff asked, perking up a bit.

Ryan shook his head. "No. Not that I could tell."

"We should be able to check her texts," I said, looking at Sheriff Baldwin. "Remember, she left her phone and purse at the cabin."

"Good point," he replied, standing up. "This could be a good lead. We should probably get back there. Hell, maybe we'll get lucky and find that she's returned to the cabin."

"Wouldn't that be nice?" I pulled my phone out of my purse. She hadn't called or texted me. As much as I wanted to be optimistic, in my heart I knew she was still missing and in a lot of trouble.

"Are we done here, then?" Ryan asked, staring up at him.

"I think so. If you remember anything else, let me know. Also, find the room number for Charlie if you can," the sheriff replied.

He nodded. "Yeah, it won't take long. Personally, I don't think he's involved."

"Hopefully, not. But, we need to question everyone who came in contact with her," I said.

The sheriff smiled at me. "You know the drill."

"We should also question the neighbors. Maybe someone saw her leave?" I added.

"You took the words right out of my mouth," said Sheriff Baldwin.

Chapter 10

Whitney

AFTER TALKING AGAIN with Sheila, and obtaining a key to the cabin, we promptly headed there. As I suspected, Brittany hadn't returned.

"Nice," the sheriff said when we walked in.

"Yeah. It is," I replied glumly, looking around.

The rustic log cabin reminded me of the ski lodge we'd stayed at when Brittany and I'd been sixteen. It had an open floorplan, a massive fireplace, a gourmet kitchen, and large windows that overlooked the lake. My first glimpse of the cabin should have been with Britt. Knowing her, she would have met me at the door with a glass of wine and a list of plans for the next few days.

"There's her purse and cell phone," Rocky said, pointing toward the pine coffee table, where a brown leather satchel sat.

I walked over, pulled out her phone, and checked the text messages.

"It looks like she'd been texting her jerk of an ex-boyfriend, Dan," I muttered, reading through them.

The sheriff walked over. "Jerk, huh? Does it look like they met up?"

"No," I said, scrolling through the texts. "He was definitely trying to hook up with her last night, though."

From their conversation, it looked like he didn't even know she was out of town.

Dan: *I miss you, baby. Why can't you come over?"*

Britt: *We already went through this before. It's over. Move on.*

Dan: *I can't. I'll do whatever it takes to win you back. I'll go to counseling. Whatever you want.*

Britt: *I'm seeing someone else. Please, leave me alone.*

Dan: *Who?*

Britt: *Nobody you know.*

Dan: *Are you happy?*

Britt: *Yes. Very.*

He didn't reply and that was the end of their conversation.

"May I?" Sheriff Baldwin asked, holding out his hand.

I handed him the phone and he began looking himself.

"*Is* she seeing someone else?" the sheriff asked.

"Not that I'm aware of," I replied.

"What's this guy Dan like?" Rocky asked, with a frown.

I told them what I knew—he and Britt had dated for a few months until she finally became tired of his controlling behavior.

"Did he ever threaten her?" the sheriff asked.

"I don't know. I think Britt would have told me. She just talked about how arrogant and self-centered he was. I'm sure he threw a fit when she broke it off," I replied.

"I'm surprised he didn't reply to her last text," the sheriff said.

"He was probably shocked that Britt replaced such a 'great catch' so easily," I replied wryly.

He smiled.

"Were there any other texts?" Rocky asked.

"Nothing from yesterday, besides her messages to Whitney," the sheriff said.

Rocky sighed.

"I'm going to start interviewing the neighbors," the sheriff said. "Then we'll head back to the lobby and see if Sheila can show us the tape surveillance from last night."

"Okay," I replied.

UNFORTUNATELY, NONE OF the neighbors were around so we headed back to the lobby. When we finally were able to see the video footage from the bar, it showed exactly what Ryan had described— Brittany having a drink and directing most of her attention to her phone. As far as the guy who'd talked to her, Charlie, the conversation between them had appeared to have been brief. Sheriff Baldwin did get his room information, however, and promised to interview him. Sheila also provided him with a list of everyone working that evening.

"What next?" I asked, the dread in my stomach growing by the minute.

"Why don't you go back to the cabin and unpack?" Sheriff Baldwin suggested. "Meanwhile, I'll get in touch with our Missing Persons Unit."

"Okay," I replied.

We talked to the sheriff for a few more minutes and then Rocky walked me back to the cabin.

"I don't know what I'm going to do if we don't find her," I said after he helped me carry my luggage inside.

"I know," he replied and then gave me a hug. "We just can't lose hope."

I nodded.

"I'm going to drive around and see if I can find her Jeep anywhere. Also, we should make some fliers," he said, scratching his whiskers. "We can post them all over town. I'll talk to Jan about that."

"Okay."

His eyes softened and he smiled sadly. "We'll find her."

I nodded. I had to believe it. It was the only thing keeping me from totally losing my shit.

Chapter 11

The Director

"THAT DOESN'T LOOK so bad, if I do say so myself," I murmured, walking around Brittany's stool and examining the haircut I'd given her. I'd tried my best to copy the style from an online photo I'd found of Janet Leigh, when she'd played Marion. I thought I'd done pretty well, for an amateur. Of course, I'd had some practice with women's hair.

My mother's.

In her later years, after her acting career had tanked, Mom became a bit of a recluse and a penny-pinching miser. Eventually, she wouldn't even leave the house, but still needed her hair trimmed now and again. I can still remember the first time she asked me to do it and how close I'd come to stabbing her in the neck with the scissors. I'd been eighteen at the time and just finishing up twelfth grade.

"It looks terrible," she complained, after I'd finished.

"What did you expect? I've never cut anyone's hair before."

She gave me a dirty look and then suggested that I go to Beauty School.

"Me? Beauty School," I scoffed. "I'm going to become an actor."

"You?" She snorted. "I've seen you act. You obviously take after your father because you're definitely not any good at it."

Her words had stung. She'd been to the majority of the plays I'd participated in and had never insulted me. On the other hand, she'd never complimented me either. Of course, I'd never asked what she'd thought, too afraid of her answer. As much as the woman had degraded me through the years, her opinion always meant something. And I'd been mostly afraid of it.

"So, he was an actor?"

I hadn't known anything about my father, other than he'd knocked her up and skipped town. She'd always refused to talk about him.

"No."

"What was he, then?"

"A loser. You'll be one too if you waste your time trying to act. Some people just don't have what it takes to succeed in Hollywood. He certainly didn't."

I'd tried getting more information out of her, but she'd only gotten angry.

"Leave me alone about your father," she snapped. "He doesn't give two shits about you. Why would you even care to know about the jerk? You're lucky I didn't abort you, which is what he'd wanted."

I'd heard that story more times than I could remember. It was always followed by how she'd had to keep me a secret, and oh what a pain that had been during her pregnancy. Mother hadn't wanted anyone to know that she'd been knocked up, so after having me, she told everyone that I was her nephew.

"Are you ready to see the new you?" I asked Brittany, pushing thoughts of Mother aside.

Brittany, who'd been compliant for the most part, didn't respond.

"Ta-da. What do you think?" I asked, holding up a large, round mirror.

She ran her hand through the bottom. "It's... so short."

"Yes, well... it will grow back. Once I put it in rollers, it will look much better," I promised, setting the mirror down. "Now, we just need the hair bleach, and then we can really get down to business."

"When are we going to actually shoot this film?"

"Hopefully, we can start tomorrow night. Are you hungry?" I grabbed the broom and started sweeping up the long strands of hair on the floor. "I was thinking about driving into town and picking up something to eat."

"Yes," she said, perking up. "I'm starving."

I knew she was also thinking it might be her time to escape.

"As soon as I'm done here, we'll get you back into the bedroom and I'll figure out what to do for dinner."

"Okay."

I looked down at her robe. She would get it wrinkled and soiled if I allowed her to sleep in it.

That wouldn't do.

I decided to let her use Amber's clothing, which I hadn't thrown out yet.

"You can't wear that to bed. You'll need to disrobe."

Her eyes widened.

I smiled. "Don't worry. I have something for you to wear."

TEN MINUTES LATER, Brittany had on the short, jean skirt and thin black sweater. She was taller than Amber, but slimmer, so the clothing hung on her.

102

"Whose were these?" she asked, not looking too pleased with the outfit.

"None of your concern. Now, get into the bed."

"Why?"

"Just do it," I ordered.

Brittany walked over the mattress and did what I asked. This time I cuffed just one of her hands to the headboard, leaving the other one free.

"I'm going to pick up some food," I explained. "Obviously, I can't let you walk around freely."

She didn't reply.

I stepped away from the bed. "I'm sure you're thirsty. Let me get you something to drink before I leave."

"Thank you."

I headed back downstairs and grabbed a bottle of water from the refrigerator, a packet of strawberry lemonade water enhancer, and two tablets of Flunitrazepam. After crushing the tablets, I added it, along with the lemonade, to the bottle and made sure it had dissolved before walking back upstairs bedroom. As I handed her the bottle, she gave me a funny look.

"Why is it pink?" she asked.

"I added some strawberry lemonade flavoring."

Brittany stared at me but didn't make a move to drink any of it.

"Go ahead. I'm not trying to poison you, if that's what you're thinking. Why would I go through all of this trouble just to kill you?"

She swallowed. "I... I would have preferred just drinking the water by itself. I try to avoid artificial sweeteners."

I bit back a smile. Artificial sweeteners were the least of her worries. "Sorry. It's the last bottle I had and the water from the faucet tastes and smells like shit."

"You know, I'm not really that thirsty," she replied, setting the bottle on the nightstand. "Thanks, anyway."

My eye twitched. "That's not true. Your lips are dry and all you've had to drink was the water from earlier. I'm not going to give you anything else, if you're going to be rude," I said coldly. "In fact," I pulled the gun out of my jacket. "I may have made a mistake, selecting you for Marion."

Her eyes lit up with fear. "Sorry. You're right. I shouldn't be so ungrateful. I'll drink it." Brittany put the bottle between her thighs and untwisted the cap.

"That's better," I said, as she brought it to her lips and began sipping it.

When she finished off one third of the bottle, Brittany put it down on the nightstand.

"Now, that wasn't so bad, was it?" I asked, grabbing the cap and screwing it back on so she wouldn't spill any by accident.

"No," she replied and smiled. "Thank you. It hit the spot."

"I imagine it did." I also knew the Flunitrazepam would kick in soon and I could leave her alone without worry.

"So, what are you hungry for?" I asked.

"I don't care. I'll eat anything."

I leaned my back against the dresser, waiting for the drowsiness to start kicking in. "Are you allergic to anything?"

"No. Thanks for asking," Brittany said, obviously trying to be my friend again. She began telling me about how she was a nurse and the number of allergy emergency situations she saw pertaining to food.

"I didn't know you were a nurse. Where do you work?" I asked, hiding my smile as her tongue began to loosen.

Brittany explained that she was an E.R. nurse at St. Michael's Hospital in some quaint little town in Michigan.

"So, you must see quite a bit of death," I said. "How fascinating."

She frowned. "Well, yes. I do. I don't know if I'd call it fascinating. It's usually pretty horrible."

I began asking her about some of the cases she'd seen and after a few minutes, I could tell she was getting very sleepy.

"That's it… my sweet Marion. Get some rest," I said, as her eyes fluttered shut. "I'll be back soon."

I BROUGHT HER back a cheeseburger and fries, forty minutes later. She was still sleeping, so I roused her. Groggy, she ate the burger eat and finished the rest of the Flunitrazepam mixture, which knocked her back out again. When I was satisfied that she was out for the night, I removed the handcuffs and put the chains back on and left.

Chapter 12

Whitney

AS THE HOURS ticked by, I became a nervous wreck. Horrible thoughts consumed me as I thought about what she might be going through. Not to mention that I couldn't eat and the thought of sleep was almost laughable. Instead of even trying, I made myself coffee and waited for some kind of news.

At around ten-thirty, I noticed that the lights were on in the cabin next door and wondered how long they'd been home. Grabbing a jacket, I walked over and knocked on the door. As I waited, a dog began to bark from inside. A few seconds later, an attractive man, with dark-blond hair and warm blue eyes, answered. He was holding a small Pomeranian dog in his arms.

I cleared my throat. "I'm sorry to bother you. My name is Whitney." I waved my thumb toward my cabin. "My sister and I are staying next door and… unfortunately, she's gone missing."

His eyes widened in shock. "*Missing?* Oh, no. You're serious?"

I nodded. "Yes. I'm wondering if you may have seen her," I held up my phone and showed him a picture of Brittany.

He squinted at the photo and shook his head. "No. I'm sorry. I've been busy working the last couple of days, so I haven't even been around much."

"Oh? Are you involved with the movie being filmed here?"

He nodded. "Yeah. I work in SFX."

"SFX?"

"Special effects."

"That's really interesting."

"Yeah. There's never a dull moment." His eyes softened. "I'm so sorry about your sister. Did she go missing around this area?"

"Yes. Sometime last night" I looked at the Pomeranian and smiled sadly. "Your dog is adorable," I said, resisting the urge to reach over and pet the dog.

"Thank you. Her name is Pixie," he said, scratching behind her ears.

"She's very, very cute."

"She knows it, too." His face became serious again. "I believe Joe may have been home all day. We should check with him."

"Thank you."

"Please. Come on in," he said, standing back.

· I hesitated, wondering if it was a bad idea. Especially since Brittany was missing. For all I knew, the neighbors could be involved. Even *with* a sweet, little dog.

Sensing my reluctance, he gave me a reassuring smile. "You're safe with us, although I totally understand if you'd prefer to wait outside. Especially with your sister missing. In fact, why don't I just go and grab Joe?"

"Thanks," I replied, relieved that he'd brought it up and I didn't have to.

"By the way, my name is Rick Gervais," he said holding out his free hand.

I shook it. "Nice to meet you."

"You, too. I'll go and grab my husband," he said.

So, they were married *and* had a sweet little dog. I suddenly felt more at ease.

I smiled. "Sounds good. Thank you."

"No problem."

He left the door open and went in search of Joe. A minute later, he returned, this time with Pixie on a leash and his husband at his side. Like Rick, Joe was also very attractive, with his dark hair, brown eyes, and easy smile.

"Hi," I said, holding out my hand. "My name is Whitney. Nice to meet you."

Joe smiled back and we shook hands.

"Sorry to take you away from whatever you were doing," I said to Joe, who bent down to untangle the dog's leash.

"Oh, I forgot to tell you, he's deaf," Rick explained when Joe didn't respond. "I told him why you're here, though."

"Ah. Okay." Pixie began sniffing around my shoes. I leaned down and began petting her. "Oh, you're so sweet. What a good girl."

"Don't let her cuteness fool you," said Rick with a smile in his voice. "We should have named her Trouble. It would have been more fitting."

I laughed.

Joe nudged Rick and began to sign.

"He'd like to see a picture of your sister," Rick said, as I stood back up. "He's been home for the last couple of days, although Joe is usually glued to his computer, writing."

His deafness also explained why he hadn't heard us knocking earlier.

"Oh, is he an author?" I asked, pulling up Brittany's picture again.

"He writes screenplays, which is how we met," Rick explained.

"How fascinating," I said, meaning it. Compared to what I did for a living, they both had such interesting careers. I turned my phone toward them so they could both see the picture.

Joe stared at the screen and frowned. He signed and then shook his head.

"He doesn't remember seeing her either," Rick said to me. "You must be going out of your mind with worry."

I nodded. "It's been horrible. Nobody has seen her since last night, when she left *Waverly's.*"

"What time did she leave the bar, do you know?" Rick asked.

"Around this time, I guess."

"And she left alone?" Rick asked.

"That's what the bartender claimed," I replied. "I just made it up here today, unfortunately. I have no idea if anyone came back to the cabin with her."

"Or if someone followed her," Rick added.

I nodded. "You didn't see anything unusual last night, did you?"

"I worked late so I wasn't around much. Let me ask Joe." He turned and began to sign.

Watching him, Joe's eyes lit up. Suddenly he began signing back frantically.

"What's he saying?" I asked, hopeful.

"He remembers seeing a Jeep leave your cabin last night, when he took Pixie out to go piddle. He couldn't tell who was driving it, though," Rick said.

"What time was that about?" I asked.

"Around ten-thirty, he thinks," Rick said.

"Thank you," I said to Joe.

He nodded.

I looked at Rick again. "If there's anything else he remembers, could you let me know?"

"Of course," he replied.

"I'm sure Sheriff Baldwin will want to question you as well," I said. "He's been helping us."

"I've never met him, but we will both do whatever we can to help," Rick said. "I just wish we could be of more help. Good luck finding her."

"Thanks."

I WENT BACK to my cabin and called Rocky's home phone. Jan answered.

"How are you, honey?" she asked, concerned.

"Trying to stay positive, although it's hard as hell. Has... has Rocky heard anything new yet?"

She sighed. "No. I take it that you haven't, either?"

112

I told her about my conversation with the neighbors.

"But, they didn't see anyone? How frustrating."

"I know."

"So, we still don't know if she left on her own or someone took her," Jan said.

"I can't imagine her leaving anywhere without her phone and purse. Not willingly. I'd bet my life on it that someone kidnapped Brittany."

Jan sighed. "I've been praying for her."

"Thank you."

"Rocky is in the kitchen right now. I'll go and get him."

"Okay."

A few seconds later, Rocky got on the phone and I told him about meeting Joe and Rick.

He sighed in frustration. "That doesn't tell us much."

"I know."

"Have you been able to talk to anyone else?"

"No. The other neighbors haven't been around much. I doubt they saw anything, anyway, if Rick and Joe didn't."

"Maybe not, but it can't hurt to keep asking around. By the way, Jan took the liberty of making some posters to hang up around town. We're offering a reward for information, too. Maybe that will help."

"A reward? How much?" I asked, curious.

"Five thousand dollars."

"Hopefully someone's memory will get jogged when they see the posters and reward offer."

"Let's hope."

I sat down on the sofa, closed my eyes, and rubbed my forehead. "Isn't there anything else we can do?"

"The sheriff said we should get in touch with the media and spread the word that way. I'm going to see about doing that in the morning. Hopefully, we can get this rolling quickly."

"Okay. Just let me know what you want me to do."

"Get some sleep. I know you must be tired from driving up here and all of the stress."

I let out a long sigh. "I'll try."

"Good. You can't be of help to Brittany if you're not thinking straight."

He had a point.

"Other than that, how are you doing?" he asked, his voice softening.

"Still just trying to wrap my head around this. I just can't believe she's missing."

"I know. And I can't believe nobody saw a damn thing. It's frustrating."

We talked a little more and then said our goodbyes.

I locked the cabin door, put my pajamas on, and then searched inside of Brittany's suitcase. When I found the flannel reindeer onesie I gave her for Christmas last year, my eyes filled with tears. I crushed it against my chest and let out a sob as I remembered how delighted she'd been with the present. As corny as I thought the gift had been, she'd squealed with pleasure and had acted like it was the best thing ever. Now, I could smell her perfume on the pajamas and it made my heart ache.

"Please be okay," I whispered into the darkness.

Chapter 13

The Director

AFTER BEING AWAY all night, I returned to the farmhouse at six a.m. On the drive over, there was a special bulletin on the radio regarding Brittany's disappearance. I suspected that they still didn't have any leads, but I knew that I'd be questioned by the police eventually. That's when my true acting abilities would shine as they always did. Thinking about it, I raised my middle finger toward the sky and the woman who'd criticized, bullied, and taunted me growing up.

"You will never be good enough," I mimicked. "Screw you, you old bat. If I wasn't good enough, I'd be dead or in prison right now. Wouldn't I?"

I could almost hear her rebuttal about how I wasn't even good enough for death.

"The Reaper doesn't want you, that's how pathetic you are," she once said to me after I tried overdosing on some of her prescription painkillers when I was fourteen. The housekeeper had been the one who found me and quickly called an ambulance. So, yeah, I'd failed. But, in time, I realized that *I* wasn't the problem in my life.

She was.

And I eventually took care of it.

WHEN I ARRIVED, Brittany was still sleeping.

I left her alone, went down to the kitchen, and pulled out my laptop. After logging in to the Dark Web, I began marketing my upcoming remake to a select group of viewers I knew would be interested. When they learned of my project, they were almost as excited as I was. I told them when I thought it would be available and they locked in their pre-orders.

BRITTANY WOKE UP two hours later. Unfortunately, she had another accident, so I made her take a shower and clean up after herself. This time

117

I brought with me an old pair of sweats and a T-shirt, which she changed into afterward.

This time, Brittany didn't apologize for the accident and I could tell she blamed me. Of course, it was nobody's fault. It couldn't be helped.

As she was pulling the plastic sheet off the bed, the doorbell rang. We looked at each other and I could tell she was thinking about bolting.

I pulled out my revolver and aimed it at her. "Don't even think about it," I said, cocking it.

"Please, let me go," she begged, her eyes filling with tears. She raised her hands in the air. "My family must be worried sick."

"I told you before, when the movie is finished, we'll be free of each other. Now, quit moving," I said, as she backed farther away from me.

"You're going to kill me, aren't you?" she asked in a hoarse voice.

"Did I say that I was going to kill you?"

She shook her head.

"I'm still wearing the mask. You can't identify me, right?"

"No," she squeaked.

"So, do what you're told. If you piss me off, however, I won't think twice about replacing you. And... if I have to do that, I will take my frustrations out on you in ways that will make you beg for death."

Her face turned pale.

"Now, enough talk. Finish up with the bed," I said sharply.

She flinched and headed back to work on the mattress.

I offered some more breadcrumbs. "Just remember, if you play your cards right, you won't have to sleep there tonight."

I could tell by her expression that she still had doubts, despite what I'd promised.

I walked over to the window and glanced outside. The person who'd rung the doorbell was already leaving in the brown UPS van.

"Good, the bleach is here," I said, turning back toward Brittany, who was eyeballing the door again. I sighed. "Don't even think about trying to escape. Your brains would be scattered all over the staircase before you made it halfway down. I don't want to shoot you, but I will if you provoke me."

Brittany shuddered.

"I've been good to you, right? I brought you food and let you take showers. I haven't raped or hurt you."

She didn't reply.

"Think about it, you're almost home free. In fact, when you're finished there," I said, pointing toward the bed, "we'll work on your hair and start filming."

"Okay."

"This will all be over soon and you'll get to see your sister again. I'm sure she's worried about you. I'll even drop you off near the resort, so you don't have to walk very far. How does that sound?"

Brittany smiled, but it didn't reach her eyes.

Obviously, she didn't believe me but was still playing nice. I knew I had to keep a much closer eye on her.

She was smarter than I thought…

Chapter 14

Whitney

I FELL ASLEEP on the sofa sometime after two a.m. and woke to the sound of my cell phone going off. Fumbling for my phone, I knocked if off the end table before answering it.

"Hello?" I asked, looking at the clock on the wall. It was almost nine-thirty in the morning. I couldn't believe I'd slept that long.

"Whit? It's me. Dad. We're at the Minneapolis Airport and will be heading to Summit Lake here in a few minutes. Has there been any more word on Brittany?"

"No," I replied, feeling the familiar heavy weight settle on my heart as I realized she hadn't returned to the cabin and was still missing. "I still haven't received any calls from her, the sheriff, or Rocky, either."

He let out a frustrated sigh. "You're absolutely sure Brittany's not with some guy and partying?"

Lillian must have put these ideas in his head. He should know his own daughter better.

"You know she's not like that. Britt is levelheaded and doesn't hang out with scumbags like—" I almost said Lillian, but knew it wouldn't help the situation, "other people we know."

"Okay. I didn't think so, but at this point, I'd almost rather she was on some kind of a bender. At least we'd know she was… alive," he replied, choking up at the end.

I softened up. It was hard on both of us. Maybe even more so on him. There was never a question on how much he loved and adored us. Despite having a shitty taste in girlfriends, he was a wonderful father. "I know. Me, too."

"If you hear anything new, call me or Lillian. Do you have her phone number?"

"Yes." I definitely had her number. "So, Lillian didn't stay behind?"

"God, no. She's just as worried about Britt as I am."

Right.

"I should get going and call the sheriff," I said, knowing that if he kept talking about his girlfriend, things might get nasty. Especially since I hadn't had any coffee yet.

"Good idea. I love you, Whitney. I know that I don't say it enough. But, you and your sister mean the world to me."

"I love you, too, Dad," I replied.

A SHORT TIME later, I called Sheriff Baldwin and we talked about my conversation with the neighbors. Unfortunately, there wasn't anything else new to report from him, but he told me that he wanted to hold a press conference as soon as possible.

"Hopefully, we'll get some leads," he added.

"When do you think the press conference will take place?"

"I'm not sure yet. I'll call you when I find out."

"Okay."

"Have you heard from your father yet?"

"Yes, actually. He called me a little while ago, from Minneapolis. He's on his way."

"Good."

"I have to ask—has *anyone* else gone missing within the last few months?"

He sighed. "We've had some runaways that have turned back up. There hasn't been any foul play, though."

It was so frustrating. No witnesses. No similar cases. Nothing but the Amber ordeal in the next town over, and she'd been killed by her crazy boyfriend. My thoughts returned to the resort. My gut told me that the answer lay here.

"Have you had a chance to interview anyone else from the hotel?" I asked him.

"Not yet. I'm heading over there shortly to talk with some of the employees who were working Friday night."

"Did you get a chance to talk to that guy in the bar? Charlie?"

"I left him a message earlier," he replied.

"Okay." I sighed and rubbed my forehead. "What about the film crew?"

"Don't worry, Whitney. We'll question and look into the backgrounds of those people, too."

"Okay."

"I have another call coming in. I'll give you a jingle when I find out what time the press conference is, or if something comes up. Meanwhile, spread the word on social media and everywhere else that you can think of about your sister."

"I will."

"Someone from our *Missing Persons* unit should be getting in touch with you soon, too."

"Okay."

After we hung up, I looked down at my pajamas and noticed how wrinkled they were. For the first time in forever, I didn't care. Fretting about wrinkles now seemed so trite. Especially with everything else there was to worry about.

"If this is your way of helping me get rid of my wrinkle phobia, it's not very funny, Britt," I said out loud.

The deafening silence in our cabin made it even more unamusing.

Chapter 15

The Director

I HAD TO bleach Brittany's hair twice in order to get it to the right shade of blonde. She was quiet throughout both processes, which made things easier. Unfortunately, there was some damage to the hair, but I knew that the camera wouldn't pick that up. And she wouldn't live long enough to worry about it.

After drying her hair, I put it in rollers and then started on her makeup. As I was applying her eyeshadow, she asked me if this was the first movie I'd ever shot.

"No. I've done others."

"How many?" she asked.

I thought back. "Twelve. This will be number thirteen." I grinned at the idea.

How had I missed that?

Many people had phobias about the number thirteen. Including my mother. Personally, it had always brought me luck. Something told me that this movie was no exception. It would be my finest to date.

"What about the other actors?" she asked.

I leaned down closer and carefully blended her eyeshadow. "What do you mean?"

"What happened to them?"

"They performed excellently."

"And lived to tell about it?" she murmured.

Noticing some of the darker powder under her eye, I wiped it away with my thumb. "We've had this conversation before."

She opened her eyes and stared into mine. "You're really going to let me go?"

If anything, she was persistent.

The woman was really getting on my nerves. Asking the same questions over and over. It must have driven her parents nuts as a child. I imagined she'd been one of those kids who begged to watch the same movie all the time.

"Why do you think I'm wearing this mask?" I reminded her again.

Brittany didn't reply.

I finished up her makeup and then made her get back into the robe. When I was through, I brought her down to the basement and began setting up my cameras in front of the shower.

"Did you demolish the bathroom just for the film?" she asked, staring at the open space that used to contain a wall.

"Yes."

I'd been lucky with it. For one, it hadn't been a load-bearing wall, so there'd been no structural damage. For two, I'd stayed clear of any pipes. As far as electrical wires, I'd managed to keep most of them intact.

"Oh. Seems like a lot of work."

"It will be worth it in the long run."

Of course, I'd have to fix the wall, but that wouldn't be too difficult. There was a YouTube video for everything and I'd always been a pretty decent handyman.

"So, you're just recreating scenes and not the entire movie?" Brittany asked.

"Yes. I don't have that much time on my hands for an entire production. So, I just focus on the most memorable parts."

"What do you do with these movies when you're finished?"

"Enjoy them. What else?"

"Oh."

She started asking more questions and I stopped her.

"Remember, the less you know… the better."

"Right."

After preparing the cameras and props, I gave her a triumphant smile. "It's time."

"To film?"

"Yes."

Looking nervous, Brittany rubbed her hands together. "Okay, what do you want me to do?"

"You're going to walk into the bathroom, turn on the water, disrobe, and step into the shower."

Brittany looked alarmed. "Disrobe? You're going to film me naked?"

"What did you think I was going to do? You can't wear the robe in the shower."

She was silent for several seconds. "Couldn't I just wear a bathing suit? Something without straps? You could just shoot me from the shoulders up?"

"I don't have one for you to use."

"But—"

I sighed in irritation. "This movie isn't about sex. I'm not going to focus it on what's under that robe. It's about art and re-creating one of the most popular scenes in history, only better."

"Better? I told you before, I'm not an actress."

"Enough. You'll do fine," I said, my patience waning.

"There has to be another way we can shoot this without me being buck-naked."

"The faster we finish this scene, the faster you're free of me and can get on with your life. Now, get over your modesty and let's do this," I said flatly.

We stared at each other for a few more seconds and then she finally relented.

Relieved, I watched as she walked over to the shower and then turned back to look at me. "Do I have any lines?"

"No. Just take a shower like you normally would, and when you see me, don't forget to scream."

"That's it?"

"Yes. Wait. There's one more thing."

I'd almost forgotten about the perfume. I pulled out the bottle of Chanel and Brittany gave me curious look.

"What's that for?"

I walked over to her. "You. Close your eyes and mouth."

"Why do I need perfume if I'm just going to wash it off in the shower?"

"Remember what I said about questions," I said icily.

Frowning, she did what I asked and I sprayed her neck with the perfume.

She opened her eyes, waved her hand in front of her face, and coughed.

"Sorry, too much?"

She wrinkled her nose. "Uh, yeah."

I inhaled deeply.

On the contrary.

It was perfect.

"Are we ready now?" she asked, looking nervous again.

I smiled. "Indeed."

Chapter 16

Whitney

DAD AND LILLIAN ARRIVED at the cabin shortly after two. As usual, she looked like a walking, talking Barbie Doll, with her perfect features, long blonde hair, and slender body. She really was breathtaking, until she opened up her mouth.

As for my father, he looked like he'd gained a few pounds since the last time I'd seen him, which had been on the Fourth of July. His face also looked flushed and ruddy, which concerned me. He'd been battling high blood pressure and diabetes for the last few years and had been trying to lose weight. He was obviously ignoring his health, which he knew better.

"So, nothing yet?" he asked sadly as we stood staring at each across the threshold.

"Unfortunately, no." I looked past him at the rain that was starting to fall again, and invited them in.

"Sorry it took so long for us to get here," Dad said, as he and Lillian stepped into the cabin. "We stopped for lunch and the service was horrible. We had to wait for almost an hour to get our food."

"I told you we shouldn't have eaten at that dump," Lillian said, removing her large framed Gucci sunglasses. "I didn't even get my water refilled until the food came. Not to mention they were out of lemon. What kind of a place doesn't have *lemon*?"

"I've eaten there before without issue," Dad said, taking off his jacket. "They were obviously understaffed today. The food was still as good as I remembered, though."

I asked them where they'd eaten.

"That place Mom and I used to take you and Brittany to on the way up here all the time. What's it called again?" Dad snapped his fingers, trying to remember it."

"*Blake's Bar and Grille*," Lillian said dryly. "Obviously not *that* memorable of a place."

"It was for us," Dad said.

I had to agree. Fond, old memories came rushing back. Mom would typically order the meatloaf, which she claimed was better than homemade. Brittany would always request a plate of Buffalo wings and a Caesar salad. The spicier the better. Dad and I usually mixed it up, although he would almost always get a burger and fries, with a strawberry malt. As for myself, I usually ordered from the breakfast menu.

"Where should we put our jackets?" Dad asked, glancing around. "Wow, Whitney. I have to say—this is a nice place. You must have paid a lot for it."

"It wasn't too bad. I'll hang your things up," I said, reaching for his jacket.

"Thanks, sweetie." He handed it to me and then helped Lillian out of her designer black faux fur coat. Sure enough, when I saw the label, I knew she had to have paid well over a thousand dollars for it.

Or, rather, my father had.

"So, how was your trip?" I asked after hanging up their things.

"Amazing," Lillian said, sitting down on the sofa next to Dad. She swung her long, blonde hair over her shoulder and grabbed his hand. "Rolly and I loved it. Didn't we?"

"It was beautiful there, that's for sure. Expensive, but I knew it would be," he said with a sigh.

"It was a trip of a lifetime and definitely worth it," Lillian said. "You should have seen the size of some of the yachts out there. They were incredible. We were able to tour a couple of them, too."

"How fun," I said, more concerned with how my father was doing. "So, you were pretty busy out there, huh?"

"Busy emptying my pockets," he mused.

Lillian snorted. "Oh, *you*. That's what you do on vacation, though, right? Spend money?"

"Some of us more than others," he replied gruffly before changing the subject back to Brittany. "Have you heard anything else from the sheriff?"

"I don't know. He's interviewing the staff and resort guests, including the people involved with a film that's being shot somewhere out here."

Lillian looked intrigued. "They're making a movie in Summit Lake? As in a major motion picture?"

I nodded. "Some kind of horror flick."

"Who are the actors?" she asked.

I told her the ones I knew about.

She looked at my dad. "Wouldn't it be something if we could meet some of them?"

He shrugged. "Honestly, I don't give two shits about the movie or those actors. I just want to find Brittany."

"Oh, I know, Rolly," she said, giving him a sympathetic smile. "Don't worry. Someone will find her."

"I sure to hell hope so," he replied.

"Can I get either of you anything to drink?" I asked. "There's water and diet soda in the fridge. Brittany filled it before she disappeared."

Dad let out a weary sigh. "Of course she did. Brittany. The organizer."

"And list maker," I reminded him.

He smiled fondly. "Her and her damn lists. She used to leave them lying all over the house. Is she still *that* detail orientated?"

I grinned. "Yeah."

"I should have hired her to be my accountant. Maybe I'd have my shit together more," he mused.

"Isn't she a nurse?" Lillian asked, looking confused.

"Yeah, and a damn good one," he replied and sighed. "You know, I was thinking that we might want to go and visit the bar where Brittany was last seen. What's the name of it?"

"*Waverly's*," I replied.

He pulled out his phone. "I'm going to call Rocky and see if he and Jan want to meet us there for drinks."

"Okay, although we might want to keep a clear head." I told him about the press conference. The sheriff had called me an hour before and confirmed that it would be at five o'clock, in front of the police station. "We're supposed to be there at four-thirty," I added.

"Okay," he replied. "I still want to go over there and check things out. That's the last place she was seen and I need to be there."

I understood exactly.

Chapter 17

The Director

I STARED DOWN at Brittany's lifeless eyes, shaking with rage. The shit had hit the fan and everything I'd worked for was lost.

Ruined.

I now had to start all over and find myself a new Marion. It simply wasn't fair.

I dropped the knife in the tub and growled in the back of my throat. I hadn't wanted to kill her, but she'd caught me off guard.

It happened while I'd been changing into my wig and dress. She'd made a run for it and had almost escaped. When I finally caught up with her, she'd kicked me between the legs and all I saw was red. I don't recall much from there, only that I somehow managed to drag her back to the basement before killing her. Once I had the knife in my hand, everything became a blur.

I looked down at my costume, which was heavily splattered with blood. I would need to replace that as well.

What a waste.

And I'd worked so hard.

I hadn't even had time to relish the life seeping out of Brittany's body during those last moments. I couldn't even remember them. As for her screams, there'd only been one and it had been uneventful.

The bitch had even taken that away from me.

My phone suddenly began to vibrate. I walked over to where I'd set it down and picked it up. My stomach knotted when I saw the text about someone named Sheriff Baldwin wanting to do interviews.

And so it begins…

Of course, I knew it had been coming.

Looking down, I let out a frustrated sigh. The problem was that I needed to get rid of Brittany's body *now*, in case the authorities tracked me to the farmhouse. I'd used a fake I.D. to rent the place and had even paid in cash. But, one couldn't be too careful.

I told the sender that I'd be there as soon as I could and then took off my costume, which would need to go into the incinerator later. After setting it aside, I placed Brittany in a plastic mattress bag and wrapped duct tape around it. When I was finished, I stared down at her.

What to do?

Normally, I enjoyed leaving my work for others to find, knowing the kind of horror it would bring to an audience. But, there wasn't time. I needed to get rid of her now and get my ass back to Summit Lake.

Grateful that I'd rented a place far from the neighbors, I lined the back of my vehicle with more plastic and placed her on top of it. I then cleaned the blood off the basement floor with bleach, took a shower, and drove to a local landfill area. Fortunately, it was a Sunday, so I had the entire place to myself.

TWENTY MINUTES LATER, after disposing of Brittany's body, I returned to my car. Having worked up a sweat, I wiped my face with a towel and took a long, refreshing drink of water while keeping an eye out for a potential witness. Luck was on my side, however. Inadvertently, so was the owner of the dump, who didn't feel the need to be open on Sundays.

Frustrated with the turn of events, but not beaten, I started the engine and headed back toward Summit Lake, where I would soon give an Oscar-worthy performance to the town sheriff, among several others.

Up for the challenge, and feeling like a little Fred Astaire was in order, I synced my iPhone with the car stereo and cranked up another oldie but goody—*The Way You Look Tonight.*

Chapter 18

Whitney

AFTER INTRODUCING MY father and Lillian, to Sheriff Baldwin, Dad asked what was being done to find Brittany.

The sheriff reiterated that they were doing everything possible to try and locate her. He'd even interviewed Charlie Whitaker already, the man who'd spoken to Brittany in *Waverly's*.

"So, let me get this straight, *nobody* saw her after leaving the lobby?" Dad asked.

"Actually, that's not completely correct," he replied, looking at his notes. "One of the desk clerks mentioned that she noticed her leaving. The woman told me she definitely left alone."

Dad sighed. "Do they have any cameras outside? Maybe someone snatched her off of the sidewalk and they caught it?"

"She made it back to the cabin. Her phone, keys, and purse were there," I reminded him. "Plus, the neighbor saw her Jeep leave late last night."

"So he says," Dad said. He frowned. "Maybe the neighbors are the ones who actually kidnapped her."

"I don't think they're involved," I said. "I met them both and they seem very nice."

"Nice doesn't prove innocence," he said gruffly.

That was true.

I looked at the sheriff. "Did you get a chance to talk with Rick or Joe?"

"Nope. Not yet."

"What about any of the other neighbors?" I replied.

"Most of them are out and about," he replied. "I left my card on each of their doorsteps with a request to call me, however."

"What about the movie crew?" I asked.

"They're being questioned as we speak," he replied. "Don't you worry, Whitney, we're interviewing every single person staying at the resort. Everyone. It just takes time."

I understood that, but I also knew that each second lost brought us farther away from finding her.

"If you'll excuse me, I need to use the bathroom," Lillian said. "Could you point me in the right direction?"

The sheriff pointed toward the restrooms.

"Thank you." She turned to Dad. "If you go into *Waverly's*, order me a Cosmopolitan, please."

"Sure," he replied.

She kissed him quickly and then headed to the ladies' room.

Dad looked at his watch. "I imagine Rocky and Jan should be arriving soon."

Just then, a female reporter, and her cameraman entered the lobby. When they noticed the three of us, they headed over.

"Hi, my name is Brenda James with *Channel Twelve News*. We heard about the woman who went missing Friday night. Is that why you're here"—she looked at his nametag—"Sheriff Baldwin?"

"Indeed," he replied.

She began asking questions and the sheriff interrupted her, explaining that he'd answer them during the press conference.

The woman looked at me. "Are you the twin sister?"

I nodded. "Yes."

"Jerry," she said, motioning toward her cameraman, who immediately began filming. She then turned back to me with a sympathetic smile. "First of all, this must just be devastating for you. When was the last time you spoke to your sister?"

"Friday evening," I replied before the sheriff abruptly cut off the questions.

"Look, I know you want to help, but now is not the time or place for this," he said to the reporter. He then told her about the press conference.

"If she's missing, shouldn't we get the story out sooner than later?" Brenda asked, looking frustrated. "Every minute is critical and it's been over twenty-four hours, if my information is correct."

"Rest assured, we're doing everything we can to find her," he replied, rocking on his heels. "Now, you're going to have to leave the resort before you're escorted out."

The cameraman stopped rolling and Brenda sighed. "Fine. We're just trying to help."

"I appreciate that, but the best thing you can do is save your questions so we can get back to what we're doing here, as well as prepare for the press conference."

"Off the record—do you believe that the movie crew staying here might hold the key to Brittany's disappearance?" Brenda asked in a low voice.

He smirked. "*For* the record—we're not ruling anyone out, including those staying or working here, as well as the people who live in town. Now, that's all you're getting out of me right now."

She looked at me again. "Good luck finding your sister," she said, her eyes softening.

"Thank you," I replied.

She nodded and the two headed back out the front door of the lobby.

"Who was that?" Lillian asked, joining us.

Dad told her.

She looked disappointed. "So, once again I missed out on being on television?"

"Really? That's all you care about?" I asked, having had enough of the self-centered woman. Ever since they'd arrived, she'd been checking her makeup, whining about getting her nails done, and talking about how she could use a massage, because she was stressed out.

"Whitney," my father scolded. "Lillian didn't mean it like that. She's just as worried about Brittany as we are."

"Right," I said dryly.

"For your information, massages are therapeutic," she said saucily. "They lower my blood pressure."

I stared at the thin, healthy-looking woman and had a hard time believing that she ever had *high* blood pressure.

"If these two don't stop bickering, I'm going to need more than a massage therapist to lower my blood pressure," Dad said to the sheriff.

The sheriff smiled.

"I told you she doesn't like me," Lillian pouted before I could reply. "That's why I didn't want to come. I knew she'd make me feel uncomfortable."

146

I rolled my eyes.

"I suppose I should get back to business," Sheriff Baldwin said. "I'll meet you guys back at the station, before the press conference."

"Sounds good," Dad replied.

As the sheriff walked away, the front door opened and this time it was Rocky and Jan stepping into the lobby.

"Finally," Dad said, looking relieved.

Chapter 19

Whitney

THE COUPLE WALKED over and Rocky gave my father a hug. The two brothers looked like they could almost be twins, accept my father had recently gained a lot of weight. Rocky, who was two years older, had actually trimmed down over the last several months; I'd learned it was because Jan had put him on a diet. She was the kind of woman my father needed. Someone who cared more about others than she did about being on television or fitting in a massage she obviously didn't need.

"Good to see you," Rocky said, stepping back and looking into Dad's face. "You look about as exhausted as I feel. I haven't slept a wink since Britt's disappearance."

"Me neither," Dad said in a haggard voice. "I still can't believe this is happening."

"I know. We can't give up hope," Rocky said. "She's out there somewhere. We'll find her."

It's what we'd all been saying, but in my opinion the words were beginning to sound hollow.

Dad nodded.

Aunt Jan gave me a worried look and then a warm hug. "So, nothing new yet?" she asked, after pulling away.

"No," I replied, noticing that Jan, who everyone thought resembled Meg Ryan, had let her curly blonde hair grow out.

I complimented her on it.

She smiled. "Thank you, Whitney. I like your new highlights" she replied, looking at my hair. "It makes your green eyes really pop."

"Thanks," I said.

Dad introduced Lillian to Jan, who she hadn't yet met, and then the five of us stepped into *Waverely's*. After ordering some appetizers and drinks, Rocky told us that they'd made fliers and had been putting some up around town.

"You offer a reward?" Dad asked.

"Yes. Five-thousand dollars," he replied. "I figured it was a good place to start."

"Indeed. Let's raise it to fifty grand, though," my father said. "I want my baby found, and something tells me that greed may be the only thing that will help get us some answers."

"You might be right," Rocky replied. "They just might not be legit ones."

"The crazies will come out of the woodwork," Dad said. "But, hopefully we'll get some legit information as well."

As they continued the conversation, I looked over by the entrance and noticed Rick and Joe walking into the bar. Noticing me, they came over immediately and I introduced them to everyone.

"Have you heard anything new?" Rick asked.

"No," I replied.

"I'm so sorry this is happening to you all," Rick said, looking around the table. "If there is anything Joe and I can do, anything at all, let us know."

"We appreciate that," I replied. "Thank you."

"Say, you're working on the movie being filmed here too, right?" Dad asked.

"I am. Joe's just really along for the ride," Rick said and smiled. "As well as to keep me sane."

"Do you think we could visit the set and meet some of the film crew?" Dad asked. "We'll leave the cast alone. I promise."

Rick's face turned thoughtful. "I don't know. I guess I could check with the director."

Lillian's eyes lit up. "That would be awesome. Is it true that Jimmy Frank is in this one?"

Rick stared at her in amusement. "Yes, he is. I take it you're a fan?"

"Definitely and I *have* to get a selfie with him," she said, her eyes gleaming. "I love that series he's in, where he plays the devil. What is that again?"

"*The Travelers*," Rick said.

She slapped her hand on the table. "Yes! That's the one."

"Honestly, when he's in the middle of filming, or on the set, he keeps to himself because it helps him to stay in character. At least, that's what I've heard. Anyway, he's staying at this resort, though. In one of the cabins. If you run into him here, you'll probably have a better shot at getting that selfie,"

"Good to know," she replied and stood up. "I have to go to the bathroom again. I'll be right back. Save my seat, Rollin."

"Of course. Hurry back," Dad said as she grabbed her purse.

She smiled at him. "If you see Jimmy Frank, don't let him leave."

"I don't even know what he looks like," Dad said, glancing around the bar.

"You don't have to. I'm sure he'll be surrounded by a crowd of adoring fans," she said.

151

"Actually, you'd be surprised," Rick replied. "He's usually incognito when he's out and about."

"But, *you'd* recognize him," she said, smiling at Rick. "So, point him out to Rollin if you see him. Please."

Rick nodded.

Lillian kissed Dad and then walked away. As she passed by the bar, I noticed a couple of guys check her out. Glancing back at my father, the two laughed and one of them said something that sounded like sugar daddy.

I sighed and looked at Joe, who was signing something to Rick.

"Joe wants to know if you'll join us for dinner later," Rick said, turning to us with a smile. "We're going to be dining at *Montecristo's*, which is on the other side of the lobby. Our treat."

The mention of the restaurant reminded me of Brittany again. We were supposed to eat there together. It brought a lump to my throat.

"That's very kind. We'd love to join you, but you don't have to foot the bill," Dad replied.

"It's no problem at all. Joe wants to do something nice for you. He feels just awful for Brittany's disappearance. Especially since he was the last person to see her."

"What do you mean?" Jan asked.

"He saw someone drive away in her Jeep," Rick explained. "He feels responsible."

"Responsible? It's not his fault at all," I said, alarmed. I looked at Joe. "How would you have even known?"

He smiled back sadly and shrugged.

"I keep telling him the same thing," said Rick. "He's like that, though. Always blaming himself when things go wrong, even when there's nothing he could have done. He's even considering doing some investigative work on his own."

"Let him. Maybe he'll get further then the police," Dad said wryly.

Joe signed something quickly.

"He wants you to know that he'll definitely do anything he can to help find your sister," Rick said. "We both will."

"We appreciate that," I replied.

Rick smiled again. "Anyway, don't forget about dinner. We have reservations at seven and want you to join us."

"We'll be there," Dad replied. "Thank you."

We all thanked them.

Rick looked at his watch. "We should go. We're supposed to meet Sheriff Baldwin for an interview. Have you seen him?"

"I think he may have gone into the banquet room," I said, remembering he'd headed in that direction.

The two men said their goodbyes and disappeared.

Rocky gave Dad a strange look. "What's up with asking for a visit to the movie set?"

"I want to see if anyone looks particularly suspicious or nutty," he said in a low voice. "Also, I didn't mention it before, but I made a call to a psychic friend of mine. Her name is Carissa Jones—"

"The woman who helps solve missing children cases?" Jan interrupted, looking excited. "I've seen her on the news. If anyone is the real deal, it's definitely Carissa."

"A psychic? Rocky asked, looking more amused than anything.

"I know you don't believe in that stuff, but this woman has a gift," Dad said. "One that can't be brushed off. At this point, I'll do anything to find Brittany."

My father had always been intrigued with the supernatural, ever since my mother had died. He'd even hired a medium once to try and communicate with her. Nothing spectacular had happened during the séance, but he'd walked away from it believing her spirit had been in the room.

"What did the psychic tell you?" I asked, not sure what to believe myself.

"Carissa said that her disappearance is related to a movie," he replied. "She also told me that she believes the person who took her is obsessed with horror films."

"Did Carissa know they were filming one of them here? I mean, it doesn't take a 'psychic' to figure out that the kidnapper might be part of the crew. You didn't pay for this information did you?" he scoffed.

"She doesn't do this for money," Dad replied.

"If she's so good with finding people, why don't you get her up here and see if she can locate Brittany?" Rocky said, taking a drink of his diet soda.

"Don't think I didn't ask. Unfortunately, she's involved with another case at the moment. She's going to keep in touch, though," Dad said. "Meanwhile, I'm not going to sit back and wait for these interviews to happen. As far as I'm concerned, we need to focus on the film crew. Hopefully, Rick can persuade the director to let us on the set."

"Yeah, hopefully," I said, taking a drink of my iced tea. At that point, I was also open to finding new ways to locate Brittany. It definitely couldn't hurt.

Chapter 20

Whitney

A COUPLE OF hours later, after dropping Lillian off at my cabin because of a sudden "headache", the four of us met Sheriff Baldwin at the station.

"Let me introduce you to Detective Andrew Parker," the sheriff said, putting a hand on the shoulder of the guy standing next to him. He explained that Andrew, who had shaggy dark hair, thick eyebrows, and warm brown eyes, was from Summit Lake's Missing Persons Unit.

"Call me Andy, please. I'm so sorry to hear about Brittany," the detective said, after shaking our hands.

"Rest assured that we're going to do everything in our power to bring her home to you."

"We hope so," Dad said. "I have to tell you, though, I feel like everyone is running in circles trying to find her without any results. It's not looking too promising where I'm sitting. Can't more be done?"

Andy nodded. "I appreciate your concern, but I promise you, we're doing all we can. It would be different if there were actually some witnesses."

"There was. The neighbor… Joe. He saw her Jeep leave in the middle of the night," Dad replied.

"Yes, we know about that. Unfortunately, that's all we have. There were no fingerprints found at the cabin other than hers. No witnesses. No other tangible evidence. Even the receptionist at the resort, the one who saw her leave, didn't notice anyone follow her out. We even checked the cameras outside of the lobby, which indicated that she walked to her cabin without incident. There's just not a whole lot to go on."

"What about the film crew?" Dad asked. "Has anyone interviewed them yet? I keep hearing it's going to happen, but when?"

"We've actually interviewed some of them," Sheriff Baldwin cut in. "And as I said, we won't leave any stone unturned."

Dad sighed and nodded. "Just don't forget about the pebbles."

Sheriff Baldwin smiled. "We most certainly won't."

THE SHERIFF BRIEFED us on what he was going to say at the press conference.

"Also, I think it might be a good idea for you or your father to say something directly to the public," he said.

"What do you mean?" Dad asked.

Detective Parker cut in. "Tell them about Brittany. She's not just a missing girl. She's a nurse who cares for others. She's a daughter. A sister. A niece. Bring her to life and let people know how special she is. Especially the kidnapper, who could be watching. He might not look at her as a real person, but a possession. He needs to know that Brittany is so much more than that."

Dad's eyes filled with tears. He looked at me. "Could you do it, Whitney? I don't think I'll be able to hold it together and get the words out."

I nodded.

I wasn't sure if I could, either, but my father was usually a man of few words. It was amazing he'd gotten into car sales and not only succeeded, but built his own company from the ground up.

"I can help, too," Jan said gently. "If you want."

"Thank you," I replied.

While Jan and I sat down to write out a plea for help in finding Britt, I overheard Detective Parker question Rocky about the meal they'd had at *Aunty K's Diner.*

"Was it busy?" he asked.

"It was when we first arrived. Do you think she could have been kidnapped by someone at the diner?" Rocky asked.

"Anything is possible. Who knows, they could have followed her back to the resort," the detective replied.

"I didn't even consider that. Good thinking, Detective," Rocky said.

"Call me Andy," he reminded him. "Now, would you be able to identify anyone who may have been in restaurant that night?"

"Maybe. I didn't really pay too much attention, although. Jan was there, too," Rocky said. "She notices more things than I do usually."

Jan, who was also listening in, told them she could certainly try to help.

"Honestly, though, we were both pretty tired that evening," Jan added. "And happy to see Britt. She had most of our attention."

Rocky nodded. "True. Plus, I'm usually in bed by nine myself," he said with a sheepish grin. "So, that was a late night for us fogies."

"No problem. Totally understandable." Andy was quiet for a while and then asked another question. "Was there anyone sitting alone or paying Brittany any special attention?"

"Not that I was aware of," Jan said.

"I didn't notice, either. Of course, we'd been catching up on things and not really conscious of anything else," Rocky said.

"Did anyone leave at the same time as you?" Andy asked.

Rocky rubbed his chin. "No. I believe that a few people left *before* us, though. A family of four and, come to think of it, there *was* another guy eating there. I didn't really look at his face or pay close attention, though."

"Nor did I," Jan replied.

"We could check credit card records and talk to the waitresses working that night," the sheriff said.

Andy nodded. "It certainly can't hurt."

"I still think you need to focus on the movie crew," Dad said. "I'm really getting a sense that someone involved with this motion picture is behind her kidnapping."

"Why do you think that?" Andy asked, staring at him curiously.

Dad sighed and then told him about Carissa Jones.

"The psychic?" Andy replied with a small grin.

"Yeah. She was pretty adamant about the kidnapper being part of the movie crew," Dad said.

"Did Brittany know anyone involved with it?" Andy asked.

"Not that we're aware of," Rocky said. "Whitney, do you know?"

I shook my head. "No. She did mention that she hoped to meet someone famous."

"But, you don't know if she ever did?" Andy replied.

I thought about our conversation on the phone and how she's been teasing me about hooking up with someone from Hollywood. I knew that Brittany wasn't like that, though.

Still…

As much as I didn't want to bring it up, I knew I had to.

"Why didn't you mention this before?" Dad asked sternly.

"It was a joke," I replied. "She's not like that. Besides, everyone saw her leave the bar alone."

Dad sighed. "True."

"What if it's someone else we haven't even considered?" Jan said. "Someone from her past?"

"You mean like the ex-boyfriend she was texting at the bar?" Sheriff Baldwin asked.

She raised her index finger. "Yes. Exactly."

"What if he followed her here to Summit Lake and pretended he didn't know where she was?" I said. "From what she told me, Dan was a manipulative guy."

"I never liked that bozo," Dad said gruffly. "He was nice around me, but I could tell there was something off about him."

"Why did they break up?" Andy asked.

I told him about how Dan had been too bossy and manipulative and she'd gotten tired of it.

"Did he ever get violent?" Andy asked.

"Not that I'm aware of. I'm sure she would have told me if he did," I replied.

"Still, we'd better follow up on that text exchange," Andy said. "Just in case."

The sheriff agreed.

THERE WERE MORE reporters at the press conference than I'd expected and they had plenty of questions, many we had no answers for. After the sheriff spoke, I read the speech Jan and I'd created about Brittany.

"My sister means the world to so many people," I finished off, choking up. "Not just her family. She's a nurse. A friend. A healer. A person who spends more time caring for others than she does herself. Please, if you have any information on her whereabouts, we implore you to help us find her before it's too late."

After I was finished, the reporters began asking questions again and the sheriff shut them down.

"I'm sorry, that's all we have for you now," he said and stepped back from the podium.

"What about a reward? We heard the family was issuing one?" someone asked.

This time, my father, who was standing next to me, cleared his throat and spoke. "Yes, we're offering up to fifty-thousand dollars for information on Brittany's whereabouts. Thank you."

"Do you think that the same person who murdered Amber Farley may have taken Brittany?" one of the reporters asked.

"He's in jail awaiting trial, right?" asked Rocky, who was standing off to the side.

"Actually, Amber's boyfriend, Tommy Smith, was released on bail about an hour ago," another reporter said. "Apparently, he has an alibi for the night she was murdered."

Shocked, I looked at the sheriff, who was frowning.

"Sheriff?" said the woman. "Is it possible we should be looking for the same perpetrator?"

"No more questions. Thank you," Sheriff Baldwin said and then led us back into the police station.

Chapter 21

The Director

I TURNED OFF the television.

So, Tommy was no longer a viable suspect. That didn't exactly fair well for me, although… I'd covered my tracks pretty well.

I imagined that someone would find Brittany's body soon. Although I'd tucked her away under a lot of debris, some idiot with his dog would eventually stumble upon her. The case would quickly turn from a missing person to a homicide, and the heat to find her killer would be turned up. Which meant if I was going to try replacing Brittany, I needed to do it quickly.

My thoughts went to the twin. It seemed fitting that she should take her sister's place. With all of the time I'd wasted with Brittany, the family owed it to me. Besides, she had the same look I was going for to play Marion.

I smiled, imagining her horror when I brought the twin to the farmhouse and told her about Brittany's last moments and how she'd begged me to spare her life. Part of me wished I'd kept her body to terrorize her. What was the sister's name?

Oh, yeah.

Whitney.

I knew it wouldn't be easy getting Whitney alone. But, I loved a good challenge and part of the fun was catching them. I just needed to find the right moment.

Chapter 22

Whitney

APPARENTLY, SHERIFF BALDWIN hadn't known about Tommy Smith. After checking into the information, he verified that it was indeed true—the man had been released and his alibi was pretty solid.

"What do you mean by 'solid'?" asked Rocky, folding his arms across his chest.

The sheriff looked up from his desk. "The night Amber was murdered, Tommy returned to *The Top Shelf Saloon* fifteen minutes after she'd left, looking for her. He ended up getting kicked out again and driving to a friend's place. Sometime after two a.m., the two knuckleheads drove back to the bar, broke in, and stole some money. From there, they bought drugs and spent the next twenty-four hours stoned out of their minds."

"And *that's* solid?" Dad asked.

"It is when there are witnesses. The friend's girlfriend is vouching that Tommy was with them, sacked out on their sofa during the time-frame in which Amber was being murdered," said the sheriff.

"And she's reliable?" I asked. "What if she's lying to protect him?"

"It's always possible, but she's a nine-one-one operator and was off duty at the time. She works directly for the sheriff's department. They apparently believe her."

I felt dizzy. "Which means that if Tommy really *is* innocent—" I put my hand against the wall to steady myself. I couldn't even say the words.

"The killer is still out there," the sheriff said in a bleak tone.

And could have my sister…

The sheriff told us he was going to call and talk to the investigative team working on Amber's case.

"They probably have a profiler who might be able to tell us something about their perp. Now, we shouldn't panic and jump to conclusions… the cases might not even be related."

From the way his eyes shifted, I knew what the sheriff believed, and it wasn't exactly what was coming out of his own mouth at that moment.

"How long was Amber missing before she turned up dead?" Dad asked tightly.

"Five days," he replied.

My father slammed his fist on the desk. "Then we still have time," he said angrily. "We need to beef up the search for her and get the FBI involved. I know you're doing what you can to help, but we need more people on this. Nobody found Amber when she went missing, and the way things are going, nobody is going to find Brittany alive, either."

The sheriff sat back in his chair and sighed. "I understand your frustration and I promise you, I'll bring everyone I can in on this case."

"I hope to damn sure you do because from where I'm sitting, things aren't looking good for my little girl," he said, loosening up this collar.

"Dad, are you okay?" I asked, noticing that his face was turning red and he was breaking out into a sweat.

"Actually, no," he replied, looking scared. "My chest feels tight. I think… I think I need a doctor."

Chapter 23

Whitney

UNCLE ROCKY, WHO was a retired paramedic, took charge right away.

"Call an ambulance," he said, moving quickly to his brother. "He might be having a heart attack."

Sheriff Baldwin put in a call, and fortunately, one arrived quickly. Rocky rode with Dad to the ER and we followed behind the ambulance. As if I didn't have enough stress, I was about to go out of my mind with worry for my dad.

This cannot be happening… I wrung my hands together.

Once we reached the hospital, he was rushed inside and quickly assessed by a doctor named Trevor Price. After taking some tests, we learned that he'd had a panic attack.

"Thank God," Dad said, looking relieved. "I thought it was a stroke or heart attack. I saw my life flashing before my eyes there for a minute."

"Your condition is actually still very serious. We'd like to keep you overnight," Dr. Price told him. "Your blood pressure is extremely high, and if we don't lower and stabilize it, you might just very well *have* a heart attack or stroke."

"I'll be okay. I don't need to stay overnight," Dad protested.

"No, you're not okay," Rocky said sternly. "This is nothing to mess with, Rollin. I know."

Dad scowled.

"Are you taking any prescription meds for your blood pressure right now?" asked the doctor.

"I was, but lost them during our trip to the French Riviera," he said, looking embarrassed. "I didn't have time to refill the prescription."

"What were you on?" Dr. Price asked, clicking the top of his pen.

Dad named off the drug and the doctor wrote it down on his clipboard.

"Can't I just get a refill and leave?" he asked.

"At this point, I'm going to have to recommend you stay overnight so we can stabilize your blood pressure and monitor you," Doctor Price replied. "I don't want to see you on the operating table, Mr. Halverson, and if we don't nip this in the bud now, that's exactly what's going to happen."

"He's right, Dad. This is something you need to take seriously," I said, putting my hand over his. "We have enough to worry about. Let's get you stabilized."

Dad sighed. "Fine."

The doctor made some more notes and then excused himself. "I'll be back shortly."

"I'll be here," Dad replied, not looking too happy about it.

When Dr. Price was gone, Dad asked if anyone had called Lillian.

"I left her a message," Jan said, standing on the other side of the bed next to Rocky.

"She hasn't called back?" Dad asked.

"No," Jan replied, pulling her phone out of her purse.

"She's probably on her way," Dad said, lowering his eyes and staring off into the distance. "Or taking a nap. She wasn't feeling well herself earlier."

"We'll go and check on her," Rocky said.

Dad nodded and looked at me. "You should also go back to the cabin and get some rest."

"No. I'm staying here with you," I said firmly. "I can rest later."

He looked at his watch and swore. "Weren't we supposed to meet your neighbors for dinner at seven?"

"It's too late now." I glanced at my phone. It was almost seven-thirty. "You're not going anywhere, anyway."

"They must think we bailed on them," Dad said. "I feel so bad."

"Don't worry. They'll understand," Rocky said. "We'll find them and explain what happened."

Dad let out a ragged sigh. "I'm sorry, guys. I'm making matters worse. We're supposed to be looking for Brittany and now I'm stuck here in the hospital," he said, looking disgusted.

"Don't be so hard on yourself," I said.

"Actually, he *should* be hard on himself," Rocky said and pointed at his brother. "You can't stop taking your blood pressure medicine. It could kill you. You should have contacted your doctor the moment you lost them so he could refill your prescription."

"It wouldn't have gotten this bad if the cops had found Brittany by now. All of this stress is what's elevating my blood pressure," he muttered.

"Maybe so, but you were already on meds to lower it for good reason," Rocky said. "You can't mess with stuff like this."

"Fine. I get it," he replied grumpily. "Lesson learned."

The doctor returned with some pills for Dad to take. Rocky and Jan then slipped away to check on Lillian and find Rick and Joe.

"You really don't need to stay here," Dad said, when we were alone together afterward. "I'm fine, you know."

"I want to. Is there anything I can get you? Like something to read from the gift shop downstairs?"

"I don't know if I could concentrate on any book right now. All I can think about is Brittany."

I nodded. I was right there with him.

"Hopefully, the press conference helped," he said, laying his head back on the pillow.

"Sheriff Baldwin said he'd keep us posted."

He sighed. "If they don't find her by tomorrow, and the FBI isn't called in, I'm contacting them myself."

I agreed that it was a good idea.

"That reminds me, I'm supposed to call the sheriff and let him know you're okay," I said. "I'll do that and go and grab some coffee."

"Okay. Can you find my phone before you leave? I'm going to try calling Lillian," Dad said.

I did what he asked and then walked out of the room, into the busy hallway. As I was heading toward the coffee machine, I ran into Dr. Price.

"How's your dad doing?" he asked me.

"Fine. Rocky gave him an earful about taking his medicine, though."

"Good."

We stopped at the coffee machine together and he volunteered to buy me a cup.

"Thank you," I replied.

"How do you like it?"

I told him with cream and extra sugar.

"You're not usually a coffee drinker, are you?" he asked with a smile.

"On the contrary. I love coffee. As long as it's sweetened, blended with ice, or in ice cream."

Dr. Price smiled and began putting coins into the machine. "I hope you don't mind me asking, but I overheard your conversation about someone missing. What happened?"

I told him about Brittany's disappearance.

He looked startled. "That's horrible. And nobody saw a thing?"

"No. Well, the neighbor noticed someone take off in her Jeep the night she disappeared. That's about it, though."

He handed me a cup of coffee. "Just don't give up hope, whatever you do. There's still a part of me that believes my sister, Tessa, will return to us someday." He looked away. "She was eleven when she disappeared."

I stared at him in horror. "And they never found her?"

He shook his head and told me she'd disappeared when he and his family had been vacationing in Summit Lake.

"I'm originally from Fargo, North Dakota. Anyway, we'd rented a cabin and had been here for about two weeks. During that time, she started hanging out with a couple of girls from town and would sometimes take off on her bike to meet up with them. One day she left and never returned."

"I'm so sorry," I replied, my heart going out to him.

"Thanks. Anyway, I know your frustration. Nobody saw anything when Tessa disappeared and she never made it to either of the girls' homes she'd been planning on visiting."

"Were there ever any suspects?"

"No. It's still an unsolved mystery as to what happened and who took her. That's one of the reasons why I moved here as an adult. I thought that maybe…" his voice trailed off and he sighed. "I don't know. I guess I feel like it's possible that she's out there somewhere and I want to be close to where she disappeared."

I had an immense urge to hug the man.

"I totally understand," I said, instead. "I'd probably do the same thing."

"What happened with your sister?" he asked and took a sip of his coffee.

I gave him the rundown of events of what we knew had occurred. Then I told him about Brittany and the type of person she was.

"She's a nurse," I added, proud of my sister. "And works her tail off."

He smiled sadly and nodded. "Personally, I think nurses are the backbone of this hospital. They do so much and are almost always underappreciated."

"It's funny you should mention that. My sister complains about it all the time."

"For good reason, I'm sure," he said. "Anyway, if there's anything I can do to help, let me know. Stuff like this hits me deeply."

I nodded. I imagined it did. Listening to his own tragic story had done a number on me, too. If I could have helped him locate Tessa, I'd have jumped at the chance. "Thank you. If there's anything I can think of, I'll do that."

"I mean it," he said, staring into my eyes. "If you need anything, even if it's just someone to talk to, I want you to call me. In fact, come with me."

I followed him over to a counter where there were business cards. He grabbed his and scribbled his cell phone number on the back.

"Here," he said, handing it to me. "Just in case."

I smiled warmly. "Thank you."

"I understand what you're going through. The uncertainty. The pain. The emotions. I was only nine at the time, but my sister and I had actually been pretty close. Not like a lot of siblings at that age. We rarely fought. Her disappearance tore me apart."

Before I could reply, I heard Lillian's voice behind me, calling my name. I turned around as she quickly approached, wearing yoga pants and a hoodie. Her blonde hair was swept up into a messy bun and she didn't have makeup on, which I had to believe was a very rare sight. I'd never seen her looking so casual.

"Is he okay?" she asked. "Rocky stopped by the cabin and told me he'd had an anxiety attack?"

I nodded. "Yes. His blood pressure was also very high because he hasn't been taking his pills."

"He's on blood pressure medication?" she asked, looking surprised.

I nodded. "He's supposed to be. Apparently, he lost his."

She frowned. "But, he's okay now?"

"We hope so," I said.

"Okay." She looked at Dr. Price, who was still standing next to me, and smiled. "Hello."

He held out his hand and introduced himself as Dad's doctor.

"It's very nice to meet you," she said, tucking a loose strand of hair back behind her ear before shaking it.

"You as well." He released her hand and then looked at the clock. "Yikes. I'd better get moving. I have another patient I need to check on." He turned back to me. "Remember what I said and don't be a stranger."

"Thank you, Dr. Price," I said, putting his card in my purse. "That's very kind of you."

"Trevor," he corrected and winked.

I smiled. "I'm Whitney, by the way," I replied, feeling a little whirl in my stomach.

He smiled back. "Let me know if your father needs anything else. We'll be monitoring him closely."

"Sounds good. Thank you," I replied.

"You bet," he answered.

"Wow, he's cute," Lillian mused as Trevor walked away. "No wedding ring, either."

I watched as Trevor stopped at the nurse's station and spoke with the older woman behind the counter. She said something that made him smile. His green eyes danced as he replied and then he glanced my way and our eyes met. I felt a flush of heat and quickly looked away.

Cute?

If you're into athletic-looking guys with killer smiles and caring demeanors, he was definitely that.

"Was he asking you out on a date?" she asked.

"No. He was just offering to help in any way he could with finding Brittany," I replied and then told her about his missing sister as we walked back toward Dad's room.

"That's a bummer," she said.

"Very much so," I replied.

When we stepped into Dad's room, a nurse was checking his blood pressure again.

"There you are," Dad said, looking relieved to see Lillian with me. "I was worried about you."

She walked over and took his other hand. "I'm fine. If anyone should be worried, it's me."

"Eh, just a little issue with my blood pressure. I'll be right as rain very soon. What were you doing? Working out?" he asked, looking at her clothes.

"I was taking a shower to get ready for our dinner with the neighbors and threw this on after I heard the news," she replied. "That's why I missed the call."

"Oh. Okay," he replied.

Considering we'd called several times, she must have been taking one long shower, I thought.

"Anyway," she squeezed his hand. "I'm here with you now."

"Yes, you are," he replied, kissing her knuckles.

"I saw the press conference on television," the nurse said as she removed the blood pressure cuff from his other arm. "I'm so sorry to hear about Brittany. Hopefully, they'll locate her very soon."

"We're praying they find her quickly or that someone will call in with a tip," Dad replied.

"No wonder your blood pressure went crazy," the nurse said. "With all of this going on. I can't even imagine."

Dad let out a ragged sigh. "It's definitely been a very stressful two days."

"I'm sure." She looked at me, and then Lillian. "Don't worry, we'll take good care of your father. He's in good hands here."

I bit back a smile.

"He's not my father," Lillian said, turning red.

Before she could elaborate further, Dad thanked the nurse quickly and then asked if there was anything to drink.

"We have water, juice, and decaffeinated tea," she replied. "What's your poison?"

"You forgot to say whiskey," he said, is eyes sparkling.

The nurse chuckled. "You wish."

"You have no idea," he said wryly.

Lillian's cell phone went off. She pulled it out of her Louis Vuitton purse and checked the screen. Frowning, she put it away.

"Who is it? More telemarketers?" Dad asked.

"No, it was just a friend," she said. "Anyway, I could use something to drink. Do you have any sparkling water?"

"There might be some in the vending machines," the nurse said.

"Oh. Okay," Lillian replied.

Dad settled on decaf tea and the nurse left to go get him some.

Dad looked at me. "Whitney, there isn't much for you to do here. Please, go back to the cabin and get some rest. Who knows, maybe your sister will even show up."

I sighed. "Okay."

"What about me?" Lillian asked, sitting on the bed next to him. "What would you like me to do?"

"Keep me company," he replied. "At least for a little while. You did just get here."

"Oh, of course. I just didn't know if you wanted to get some rest yourself," she replied. "You know how much I hate hospitals, and if you're sleeping, I won't have anything to do."

I rolled my eyes.

She saw it and gave me a dirty look.

"Don't worry. I doubt I'll be sleeping for a while," he said.

"Okay. Good," Lillian said. "Maybe we can talk about New Orleans again."

"I can't even think about another trip with Brittany gone, Lillian," he said with a sigh.

"I have to visit my sister, though. She's having her baby soon," she replied.

Although I really wanted to say something salty to Lillian, I managed to hold it back. Instead, I gave Dad a hug and then promised to report anything new.

"Okay. And for heaven's sake, be careful out there," he warned. "I don't know what I'd do if anything happened to you, too."

I knew how he felt. For a second, I'd thought I'd lost my sister *and* my father. Still, even he wasn't out of the woods, yet, I gave him a reassuring smile. "I will."

"Don't forget to apologize to your neighbors again for me. In case Rocky didn't get a chance to."

"I'll talk to them." I finished up my coffee and threw the Styrofoam cup away. "Do you know how to get back to the cabin, Lillian?"

"I drove here. I'm pretty sure I can figure it out," she said briskly.

"Sorry," I replied, realizing she was still mad at me about the eye roll. "I just wanted to make sure. It's easy to get lost out here."

"Our rental has navigation," she replied.

I directed my attention to Dad. "I'll call you later."

"Thank you."

I slung my purse over my shoulder and walked out of the room. As I began walking, I heard Dad chastise Lillian about being nicer and wondered how long it was going to be before he opened his eyes and

182

realized that having an expensive trophy girlfriend wasn't worth it.

Chapter 24

Whitney

MY STOMACH WAS growling on the way back to the cabin, so I pulled into a Culver's drive-thru and purchased a cheeseburger and a small caramel turtle shake.

"Please pull up to *Lane 1* and we'll bring your food out shortly," the young man said, handing me my shake along with a blue numbered sign to hang on my window.

I thanked him and moved my car forward. As I was waiting, I noticed two teenage girls sitting inside, joking and laughing together at a table. Of course, it brought back more endearing memories of Britt and

I, so, I started getting a lump in my throat followed by a couple of tears.

Taking a shaky breath, I pulled down my visor and started dabbing at the moisture under my eyelashes. It was then that I suddenly had an intense feeling of being watched. I turned to look out the passenger window and found a man, in a silver Mercedes Benz E-Class, parked across from me. I assumed he was a customer, but he didn't have a plastic order number hanging on his window. In fact, they were all up and tinted, so I couldn't make out his face. I could tell he was still staring at me, however, and longer than necessary.

A little weirded out, I turned away just as one of the Culver's employees walked up with my cheeseburger.

"Here you go," the teenager said, handing me a small bag. "Have a nice night."

I thanked him and told him to do the same.

"Thanks."

The employee grabbed the number and I rolled my window back up. As I was pulling out of the lane, I noticed the man in the Mercedes still staring at me from his parked car.

Brushing it off, I left the parking lot and began driving toward the resort. After a couple of stop signs, I reached a red light and waited for it to turn green. As I sat there, headlights approached from behind and I noticed, in dismay, that it was the guy in the Mercedes. This time I could see him a little better, and noticed he was wearing sunglasses, which was odd for this time of night.

The light turned green and I continued on my way, keeping an eye on the road as well as the stranger behind me. As the blocks turned into miles, and I noticed he was still behind me, the warning bells in my head began to blare. Then, when I turned into the entrance of the resort, and he pulled in after, I knew I wasn't being paranoid. He was either following me, or another guest.

A very *strange* guest.

Regardless, I knew going back to my cabin wasn't a good idea.

Trying to remain calm, I pulled my vehicle up to the valet service, in front of the main lobby. I parked my car, got out quickly, and looked toward the Mercedes, which was driving past the lobby very slowly.

"Do you have dinner reservations or staying at the hotel?" the valet asked, getting my attention.

I turned to look at the baby-faced young man, who looked around nineteen or twenty. "I'm sorry. I'm actually staying at one of your cabins." I told him about the man I thought might be following me.

His eyes widened. He looked past my car. "Is he here?"

"He just passed by in a newer silver Mercedes E-Class," I replied, pointing in the direction of where the car had gone.

He walked past the pillar, searching for the car. Not seeing the vehicle, he walked back. "Are you sure this guy was following you and not just another guest?"

"Honestly, he *could* be. I just felt funny about the whole thing." I then told him about my sister disappearing.

"Oh, that was *your* sister?" he replied.

I nodded.

"Did you find her yet?"

"No."

"Damn." He looked toward the service road, where headlights were approaching from the direction of where the Mercedes had disappeared.

"There he is," I said, my pulse racing as the car drove past us, this time at a much quicker pace. He took a right out of the parking lot and disappeared down the road.

"You're right. He's following you," the valet said, looking at me.

"So, I'm not just being paranoid?"

"I don't think so. His license plate was missing and that's a definite red flag."

Chapter 25

Whitney

I WENT INTO the lobby and talked to the manager on duty, which was once again, Sheila. I explained what had happened and she stared at me in horror.

"You should call the police," she replied.

"I'm going to. I was wondering… is there any way that I could move to a different cabin? I really don't feel safe in the one I'm at."

"I don't blame you. Let me see what I can do." She turned to her computer and began typing away. After about a minute, she sighed and shook her head. "I'm sorry. We're totally booked. Unless, you'd rather stay in the hotel? We have a few rooms available."

I thought about Dad and Lillian. They also needed a place to sleep. I explained that they were staying with me while the police searched for Brittany.

"I understand and no problem," Sheila said, typing on the keyboard again. "I can get you adjoining rooms. No upcharge, of course."

Our cabin had been twice the amount of the rooms, so I knew she wasn't exactly doing me a huge favor. As if reading my mind, she mentioned the price difference herself.

"Tell you what, we have two *suites* available, down the hall from each other. They're much nicer than the regular rooms. I'll swap you the cabin for two of those."

"I think that'll work just perfectly. Let me just check with my father first, though," I replied.

"No problem. Take your time."

I called Dad's cell phone. Because I knew he'd worry and probably leave the hospital, I didn't tell him about being followed.

"I just don't feel totally safe in the cabin," I said to him, which was the truth. "Who knows if this guy will return and try breaking in?"

"To tell you the truth, I was a little worried about that myself. Since I'm not around, I think it would be better for you to take the manager up on the offer. You just never know."

"Okay. I'll set it up then."

"Okay. Lillian will be leaving here shortly, too. She has a headache again and wants to get some rest."

"Okay. Tell her to meet me at the hotel lobby and to park by the valet service."

"Sounds good. What about all our luggage?"

"I'll see if they can send someone with me to bring it over," I replied.

"Okay. Sounds good," he replied.

I hung up and told Sheila that we definitely wanted to switch to the suites.

"Great. I'll have security escort you back to pick up your things."

I sighed in relief. "Thank you."

As we were finalizing everything at the counter, I noticed Joe and Rick walk out of *Montecristo's*.

"Could you excuse me for just a second?" I said to Sheila.

"Sure."

I hurried over to the two men and began apologizing for missing dinner.

"No need to explain," Rick said. "Rocky and Jan found us earlier and told us what happened. How is your father doing?"

"Not too bad. He just needs to be more responsible with his pills and quit being such a stubborn fool," I replied, smiling weakly.

"Parents can be so frustrating at times," Rick replied. "By the way, has there been any progress with your sister?"

"No, unfortunately." I then explained that I was moving to the hotel and about being followed.

"Seriously? Have you reported it to the police yet?" Rick asked, looking concerned.

"No. I suppose I'd better," I replied, biting my lower lip.

He put his hand on my shoulder. "You know, this could be the same person who took your sister. You need to let them know right away. Did you get a license plate?"

I shook my head. "It was missing from the car."

Rick's eyes widened. "Now that's definitely a bad sign. Call and report this."

Joe, who'd been standing there silently, began to sign and Rick answered him.

"He's worried about you, too," Rick said, when they were finished. "And thinks it's a great idea that you're moving to the hotel."

"It's not an easy thing to do," I admitted. "I keep thinking—what if she comes back and I'm not there?"

"Your sister will probably go to the police if she gets away from whoever has her," Rick said. "Or call you, I'm sure."

Joe began to sign again.

"He's saying that we'll keep a watch out for her too, while we can. If we see her, we'll make sure she knows where you are."

I smiled. "Thank you."

AFTER TALKING TO them for a few more seconds, and exchanging phone numbers, I hurried back to Sheila, who was patiently waiting for me.

"Sorry," I said. "I wanted to fill them in on what was happening."

"You don't have to explain anything to me," she replied and then handed me our new room keys and an envelope with our paperwork. "Sam and Doug will be helping you move your items. They should be here in a minute."

"Thank you."

Chapter 26

Whitney

FORTUNATELY, IT DIDN'T take too long to get all our things moved from the cabin to the suites, which were also very rustic and of similar design. The two gentlemen who assisted me were very nice and made everything so much easier.

Afterward, I called Sheriff Baldwin and left him a message, telling him about the guy in the Mercedes. He returned my call within a few minutes.

"So, he actually removed the license plate?" the sheriff asked.

"Yeah."

"Do you know if he had one when you were at Culver's?"

"I'm not sure. I didn't really notice back then."

"I'm just curious as to whether or not he didn't have one the entire time, or if he took it off after reaching the resort. It's also possible that he's driving a stolen vehicle. I'm at home right now, but I'm going to call this in and see if there are any reports of missing vehicles matching the Mercedes."

"Okay. Do you know if anyone has responded to the press conference yet?"

"We've had some nutcases call in with bogus information to try and collect on the reward."

"Are you sure what they're giving you is bogus?"

He chuckled humorlessly. "Yes. One person said she was abducted by aliens and he was witness to it. Another swore that she'd run away to join the circus."

I groaned.

"We usually get all kinds of crazies calling in with 'tips' like this, so it's nothing new."

"I bet."

"Don't worry, Whitney. The moment that me or Detective Parker learn anything new, you'll get a phone call."

"Thank you."

AFTER GETTING OFF of the phone with Sheriff Baldwin, I received a text from Lillian, who I'd forgotten about. She was down in the lobby and looking for me. I gave her my room number, and within a few minutes, she was at the door.

"Sorry," I said. "There's been so much going on, I forgot to look for you."

"It's okay," she replied.

"All of your things are in the suite down the hallway," I said. "I'll show you."

We walked silently together to the other room.

"How's Dad?" I asked as I opened up the door for her.

"He's doing fine."

"Good." I handed her two key-cards. "If you need anything, you know where I'm at."

She yawned and thanked me.

"Uh, if you want, we can drive together to pick Dad up tomorrow."

"Sure." She suddenly reached over and put a hand on my forearm. "Look, I know that things have been a little tense between us. I'd really like it if we could be friends, though. Especially, for Rollin."

I sighed. She was right and Dad needed my support. Both of us were stressed out, but he definitely couldn't afford to worry about me and Lillian not getting along. "Yeah. Okay."

She looked relieved. "Maybe we could have brunch tomorrow?"

"Sure. We could do that before picking up Dad. Did anyone there mention what time they'd be releasing him?"

"Not to me."

"Okay, I'll call and find out in the morning."

"If it's too early, maybe we could settle for lunch?" She smiled sheepishly. "I'm not exactly a morning person."

Big surprise there.

"Sure. I'll let you know what the hospital says in the morning," I said, pushing my snarky thoughts aside. At least she was trying.

"Sounds good."

Lillian suddenly gave me an awkward hug.

"I hope they find Brittany," she said softly before releasing me.

"Yeah. Thanks. Me, too," I replied, warming up to her a little more. I stepped out of the room. "Goodnight."

"Goodnight."

I FELL ASLEEP shortly after eleven and woke early to the sound of someone pounding on the door. Startled, I put on the white complimentary hotel robe I'd found on the bed and hurried to the door. I looked through the peephole and saw Sheriff Baldwin and Rocky standing on the other side.

I threw the door open. "What's going on? Did you find Brittany?" As the words left my lips, I noticed the somber expressions on their faces and took a step back. "What is it?"

"Can we come in?" Rocky said.

Noticing that his eyes were red-rimmed, I knew what they had to say was bad. Tears filled my eyes as I stepped back. "Sure."

Rocky closed the door behind him and then put his arm around me.

"I don't know how to say this," Sheriff Baldwin said, removing his hat. "But—"

"Wait," I choked, putting my hand on my chest. My heart felt like it had shattered into a million pieces and he hadn't yet even said the words I knew were about to leave his lips. "Don't... say it. I can't... I don't want to know."

The sheriff looked at Rocky, not sure what to do.

"I'm sorry, kiddo," my uncle said, pulling me into his arms. "Brittany... they found her. She's... gone."

"No!" I wailed, burying my head into his chest and sobbing.

She was dead.

Gone forever.

My best friend in the world.

My beautiful, loving Britt.

My heart felt like someone had wacked it with a sledgehammer, and at that moment, I wanted to die myself.

"I know. I know," Rocky said, holding me tightly. He too began to cry. "I'm... so... sorry."

Chapter 27

Whitney

IT TOOK ME some time before I could collect myself and listen to the rest of what the sheriff had to say.

"She was found in a landfill area over in Bear Creek," he explained softly as we sat across from each other on the sofa.

"How did she die?" I asked, grabbing another tissue from the coffee table between us.

He let out a ragged sigh. "We don't know the exact cause of her death yet. That will determined by the medical examiners, but… she was obviously murdered."

I could tell by his expression that he was holding a lot back. I couldn't blame him for hesitating, either. Not after watching me fall apart before I'd even heard any of the details.

"Was she killed like... Amber?" I asked hoarsely. I didn't want to know the grisly details, but knew I needed to. Before it was all over the news. "The same way?"

"All I know is—" he hesitated again, looked at Rocky, and then me again—"she was stabbed."

Imagining what she must have gone through, the sheer terror and pain, made me start crying all over again.

"Somebody better find this guy. He needs to pay for killing my niece!" Rocky growled, putting his arm around my shoulder again to comfort me.

Sheriff Baldwin nodded. "The FBI is also involved and we are not going to stop searching for this asshole until he's found and behind bars. I swear to you."

"I know you mean well, Sheriff, but if it turns into another fiasco like the one that happened a few months ago with Jan's daughter, I'm getting involved," Rocky replied.

Sheriff Baldwin scowled. "Now, Rocky, just like I told you last time, you can't act like some kind of vigilante. You're either going to hurt someone innocent, or become a victim yourself. Not to mention that you could end up in jail."

"If it stops another young woman from getting murdered, I can live with that," he said flatly.

The sheriff shook his head, but didn't reply.

I reached over and grabbed another tissue. "Does it look like it might be the same person who killed Amber?" I asked, after blowing my nose.

"As far as I'm concerned it is. Too much of a coincidence," Sheriff Baldwin replied. "They're still gathering evidence, however, so we'll know from the M.O. Hopefully, this freak left behind something more incriminating."

"Amber was last seen at a bar in Bear Creek. My sister went missing after visiting *Waverly's*. That's a pretty obvious common denominator. Can you check the credit card receipts of these two places and see if someone visited both?"

The sheriff nodded. "Most definitely. We've already got someone checking into that."

"Do you think this guy lives in Bear Creek or is just using it to throw everyone off?" Rocky asked.

"From what I know, most serial killers don't like to leave their victims too close to home," he replied. "But, there's going to be a profiler looking into both cases and they'll have a better answer for us soon."

"Does Dad know about her yet?" I asked softly.

"No," Rocky said. "We haven't been to the hospital yet."

"We shouldn't wait any longer," I said, standing up. "If he finds out about this on the news, it will be bad."

"I agree," the sheriff said.

"At least he's in the hospital," Rocky said in a grim voice. "When he finds out, this could kill him."

Chapter 28

Whitney

BEFORE WE LEFT, I called Lillian and told her the news.

She gasped. "Oh, my God. How, awful! When did they find her?"

"A few hours ago, I guess. Anyway, we're heading over to the hospital to tell Dad. I'm sure he's going to want you there." I sniffled.

"Yes. Of course," she said. "Would it be okay if I met you there? I just got out of the shower."

"Sure."

After hanging up with Lillian, Sheriff Baldwin drove us to the hospital.

"Where's Jan?" I asked as we pulled into the parking lot.

"She had an early meeting with some parents. She couldn't get ahold of them, so she went in. She's meeting us here, though," he replied.

Jan was an elementary school teacher.

"No problem."

When we arrived, she was already waiting for us in the lobby.

"I got here as fast as I could." She pulled me in for a hug. "I am *so* sorry, Whitney."

"Me, too," I said, trying not to cry again.

She pulled away and looked past us. "Where's Lillian?"

"She's going to meet us here," I replied.

"Should we wait for her?" Rocky said, scratching his chin and looking toward the hospital entrance.

"No. With our luck, he'll hear the news before we have a chance to get to him," the sheriff said, looking at his watch. "It's probably already on the news."

I groaned.

Luckily, when we arrived in Dad's room, he was already up and hadn't heard anything.

"I couldn't sleep on this rock-hard hospital bed. I'm surprised you're all here this early. Are they kicking me out?" he asked with a grin.

"Hopefully, soon. What are you doing?" I asked, noticing that he was holding his phone.

"Playing *Candy Crush*. I haven't played this game in so long. Now I can't seem to stop," he said, his smile fading as he looked at my face. "You've been crying. What's wrong?"

I tried telling him, but was too distraught and couldn't get the words out.

"Wait a second. Is this about Brittany?" he asked, his voice breaking. "What's going on? Tell me."

Rocky put his hand on Dad's shoulder. "I don't know how to say this, Rollin, but… they found her. She's…" He couldn't continue either without crying. "She's gone, man. Someone killed her."

Dad's face turned red and his eyes filled with tears. He looked at Sheriff Baldwin. "My little girl was murdered?!"

The sheriff nodded.

Shaking with rage, Dad pointed at him. "This is your fault! If you would have been doing a better job trying to find her, none of this would have happened!"

Sheriff Baldwin remained calm, although I could tell he was horrified by Dad's words. "Sir, we did everything we could. There just wasn't—"

"Enough with the excuses!" he hollered. "Now, get the hell out of my room before I get out of this bed and kick your good-for-nothing ass!"

I gasped. "Dad!"

"It's okay. I'm leaving," Sheriff Baldwin said, backing away. "I'm sorry for your loss."

Dad gave him the finger.

The sheriff looked at Rocky. "I meant what I said—I'm not resting until I find the man who murdered her."

"Just like you promised to find her," Dad growled before Rocky could respond. "I'm not holding my breath."

"I'll call you when I have more news," Sheriff Baldwin said to me before putting his hat on and walking out of the room.

Dad looked at me, and that's when he really lost it. "What are we going to do without her?" he asked, crying.

I leaned toward him and we hugged. "Find the person who did this. For Brittany."

Chapter 29

Whitney

IT TOOK QUITE a while for Dad to calm down and of course, his blood pressure skyrocketed from all of the stress.

"Where in the world is Lillian?" Jan asked when the two of us were alone, outside of Dad's room. We'd been there for almost two hours and she had yet to arrive.

"The last time I spoke with her, she was just getting out of the shower."

She looked down the hallway, toward the lobby. "Do you think we should be worried?"

I followed her gaze and chewed on my lower lip. *Should* we be worried about her?

My dad had complained, more than once, about how long it usually took for the woman to get ready. In normal circumstances, I would have thought it was just her being her. But, there was a killer running around. Yeah, it was in the middle of the day, but who knew what this nut was capable of.

"I'll try calling her when we get back into the room," I replied.

"I'm surprised your father hasn't said anything about her absence."

"He has so much on his mind already. He probably hasn't noticed she's running late."

"Yeah. I'm sure."

WHEN WE RETURNED to Dad's room, the doctor on duty was just finishing up with him.

"Well, can I leave *now*?" he asked the older, gray-haired man named Dr. Thayer.

"I think we should keep you around a little longer until I'm happier with those numbers," he replied.

"Oh, for God's sake," Dad huffed.

"It's for your own good," the doctor said patiently. "I know you're frustrated, but try and relax. Or, you'll be spending another night here for sure."

Dad sighed. "So, I should be able to leave later?"

"I think you should be free to go, as long as we can stabilize your blood pressure. It's looking better, just not where we'd like it to be," he replied.

"Okay. Did you hear that? I should be able to leave today. You heard him," Dad said.

"Hopefully. I'm not making any promises. It depends on what the numbers say. We'll adjust your prescription a little and see if that helps," he replied.

"Okay," Dad said.

There was a knock at the door and Lillian peeked her head in. "Are you decent?" she asked with a smile in her voice.

"It's about time you showed up," Dad replied. "I was about to send Rocky out to make sure you were okay."

She walked in carrying a bouquet of brightly colored flowers. "I know. I'm sorry. I got hung up at the florist."

"You didn't have to buy flowers," he said.

She put the vase down next to him on the end table and then kissed him on the lips. "I know. I just wanted to do something to cheer you up. How are you doing?"

He let out a shaky sigh. "Devastated. We all are," Dad said, looking at me and then Rocky and Jan. "I keep hoping that this is just a nightmare and none of you are really here."

We all agreed.

Lillian sat down next to him on the bed. "I'm so sorry, Rolly. I know this must be so hard. I can't even imagine..."

They all started talking about Brittany, and after a while, I couldn't listen any more. My heart ached so much, I had to get out of the room.

"I'll be back. Does anyone want anything to eat?" I said, walking toward the door with my purse. "I'm going to the cafeteria."

"I'll come with you," Rocky said. "Anyone else want anything? We can bring something back."

"I'll take a sandwich if they have one. You know what I like," Jan said.

"Sure. Lillian?" he asked.

"I had breakfast before I got here," she replied.

My eye twitched. Here, Dad was having one of the worst days of his life and she'd found time to grab breakfast and get flowers. From my father's expression, he was looking a little miffed himself.

We walked out of the room and headed down the hallway.

"Can you believe Lillian?" I muttered. "She took her own sweet time getting here. I'm surprised she didn't get her nails and hair done, too."

Rocky chuckled. "Yeah. She's something else. Sometimes I even have to wonder what the hell he was thinking. She's a twit."

"I don't think she's as dumb as she wants us to believe," I replied. "I think she's just totally self-centered and incapable of any true empathy for others. Yeah, she says the right things when she needs to, but come on. If she really cared about Dad, she wouldn't have even *left* the hospital last night. She was there for maybe an hour."

He sighed. "Some people really don't like hospitals. Anyway, you never know. She might have real feelings for him."

I snorted. "Do you really believe that?"

He smiled wryly. "Not really. I'm going to pretend, though. I'm already annoyed at enough people as it is."

After grabbing some food from the cafeteria, we headed back to the room. As we stepped inside, my cell phone began to ring.

"Oh, it's Rick," I replied, looking at the screen. "He must have heard the news. Hello?"

"Hi, Whitney. I'm sorry to bother you, but I wanted to let you know that I talked to the movie director about your situation and he's agreed to let you and your family visit the set. Hopefully, it will cheer up your dad a bit. How is he doing, by the way?"

He hadn't heard the news.

"Actually, not so good." I told Rick about what we'd learned and he gasped in horror.

"I am *so* sorry for your loss," he said softly. "Is there anything that I can do?"

"No, but thank you."

"If you ever need anything from me or Joe, don't be afraid to ask." He sighed. "I wish I could give you a big hug right now. My heart is breaking for you."

"Thanks, Rick," I replied, my bottom lip wobbling.

"I'll let you go. I'm sure you just want to be with your family and talk about all of the loving memories. I'll pray for you guys."

"Thanks."

"Take care and call me if you need to talk. I know we're strangers, but… I've found that sometimes, they're the best listeners."

"Thank you, Rick. I appreciate that."

We exchanged a few more words and then hung up.

"What did he have to say?" Dad asked.

"He was obviously shocked." I told him the news about the director allowing us to visit the movie site.

Dad nodded. "Good. Set it up."

"You don't still believe it's someone involved with that film?" Rocky asked.

"Your damn right I do," he replied. "I told you that from the beginning."

"Because of the psychic?" Rocky said dryly.

He nodded. "It makes sense, doesn't it? She said the kidnapper liked to film his victims. Both murders happened while they've been in town. There's been nothing else like this in Summit Lake, right?"

"You have a point," Rocky said.

"Shouldn't we leave the investigating to the sheriff?" Jan asked.

"We already did. Look where that got us," Dad said angrily. "Rocky, I say we accept the invitation and do our own 'investigating'."

He nodded. "Sounds good to me."

I wasn't sure it was a good idea myself. I knew they meant well, but they could either help or really hinder the investigation. Badly. I tried telling them this, but the two men were stubborn and refused to listen.

"If we don't find this guy, there will be more victims," Dad said. "At the very least, we might be able to shake things up and cause the bastard to make a mistake."

"He's right," Rocky said. "Don't worry, Whitney. Your Dad and I aren't going to do anything stupid. We just want to meet these people and see if something seems 'off' about one of them."

"I think that's a great idea," Lillian said.

Her acknowledgement only reconfirmed to me that it definitely… wasn't.

Chapter 30

Whitney

AFTER CALLING RICK back and letting him know that Dad still wanted to visit the movie set, to "take his mind off of things" I also decided to do a little 'investigating' myself.

"What was the name of that bar where Amber was last seen?" I asked Rocky, when we had a minute alone. "The one in Bear Creek."

"*Top Shelf Saloon*, I believe," he said. "Why?"

"I'm curious about it and was thinking of taking a ride," I replied.

His expression told me he didn't much care for the idea. "To check it out?"

I nodded. "Yeah. Who knows, maybe the killer is a regular."

He shook his head. "You heard the sheriff. Usually these killers don't murder in their own backyards. If you ask me, that's the last place you'd find him. Especially now with Brittany being…" he couldn't get the rest out.

"Or, maybe he's so cocky and arrogant, that he believes nobody will ever catch him so he goes back to gloat."

"True," he replied, looking disgusted.

"I think it's worth checking out. Especially at night."

He sighed and rubbed his hand over his face. "I don't know. We don't even know if he picked her up from the bar or on the road. Apparently, she lived only a couple blocks away from it. He could have just been driving by and decided to kidnap her."

True. Still, I had an urge to see the bar. I felt like Amber and my sister now had a real connection and I wanted to know more about the poor woman. I explained my feelings to Rocky.

"Look, I understand. I just don't think it's a good idea for you to be hanging out at a place like *Top Shelf Saloon* to begin with, let alone when there's a serial killer on the loose."

"Come with me."

He frowned. "How did I know that was coming up next?"

I put my hands together. "Please?"

Rocky looked away for a few seconds and then nodded. "Fine. Something tells me if I don't go with you, you'll just take off on your own, anyway. You're stubborn. Just like your dad."

I grinned. "And don't forget my brave, handsome uncle."

Rocky snorted.

WE AGREED THAT he'd pick me up around ten o'clock p.m. to visit the bar. We also agreed not to tell Dad. He already had enough to worry about. Not to mention, Rocky thought it might draw more attention to us if we walked in as a group of three.

"Are you going to tell Jan?"

"Of course. That woman keeps a tight leash around me," he joked.

"And you wouldn't have it any other way, would you?"

"Nope."

My cell phone went off just as we walked back into the room. It was Rick.

"I got your message. Just call me when you're ready to visit the set. We usually get here by eight a.m."

"Thanks, Rick. Where are you filming?"

He gave me directions to an area on the west side of Summit Lake.

"It probably won't be until tomorrow or Wednesday," I said.

"No problem. Just call me beforehand so I can look out for you. There's a lot of security, as you can imagine."

"I understand."

After hanging up with Rick, I told everyone about the conversation.

"Oh, how fun!" Lillian said, looking excited.

"Remember, we're not going for the 'fun' of it," Dad grumbled. "We're trying to find Brittany's killer."

"I understand that," she said with a frown. "But, it's still exciting to see people from Hollywood." Lillian walked over to the mirror and checked her makeup. "Maybe they're in need of some extras, too. You just never know."

"No, I guess you just don't know when the killer is going to strike again," he replied dryly. "That might open up a spot for you."

She gave him a dirty look.

DAD'S BLOOD PRESSURE eventually began to stabilize, which was a big relief to everyone.

"When can I leave?" he asked one of the nurses, after she checked his number again."

"Let me go and find Dr. Price," she said, folding up the cuff.

"He's back?" I replied, perking up a little.

She smiled and nodded. "He just started his shift again."

After the nurse left the room, Lillian gave me a knowing smile. "That's the dreamy doctor you were talking to yesterday, right?"

"Yes," I said, suddenly feeling very defensive. This wasn't exactly the time to be thinking romantically about anyone, including doctors.

"Dreamy, huh?" Dad said. "What am I? Chopped liver?"

"Silly," Lillian said, sitting down next to him. "You are definitely not chopped liver. Anyway, I think he likes Whitney.'"

"That's ridiculous," I mumbled.

Dad looked at me sadly. "You're beautiful, Whit. I'm sure he's noticed."

Just then, Dr. Price walked into the room holding Dad's medical chart.

"So, how are we doing today?" he asked, looking at the clipboard. "Feeling calmer?"

"I don't know about that," Dad said bitterly and looked at me. "I guess he hasn't heard."

"Heard what?" he asked looking up from the chart.

I told him about Brittany. When I was finished, he couldn't believe it either.

"I am so sorry for your loss," he replied, looking stunned. "You all have my deepest sympathies."

"Thank you," I replied.

"Have you been down to the morgue to identify her?" he asked. "You know, to make sure it's her?"

"Not yet," I replied.

"We're waiting for the call," Rocky said sadly.

He nodded. "You know, we have a crisis counselor, and a chaplain, on staff, if anyone is interested."

"Thank you," I replied. "We'll keep that in mind."

"We have each other," said Dad, holding Lillian's hand and looking at me. "We'll... get by."

"There's no substitute for family," he said. "If you change your mind, however, Father Bartlin is a good guy."

"We appreciate that, Doc. Not to change the subject, but... when can I get out of here?" Rocky asked.

"I think I can give you the green light," he replied, looking at the chart again. "But. I'm going to send a monitoring cuff with you and I want you to record your readings, okay? If it starts to go up again, you'll need to give us a call."

"Will do. Thank you," Dad replied, looking relieved.

"And I guess I don't have to tell you how important it is to keep taking your pills?" he added.

"Nope. I'll take them religiously and if I happen to lose them again, I'll get on the horn and call you or my primary doctor," Dad replied.

"Good. Then, let's get you released. I'm sure you're tired of seeing this place," Dr. Price said.

"You have no idea," Dad replied.

AS WE WERE pushing Dad in a wheelchair, which was standard procedure, toward the front doors, Dr. Price pulled me aside and asked if I wanted to have a drink with him in the next few days, which caught me off guard.

"I figured you might want to talk. I know you're busy, though, with everything going on. So, if you can't, or don't want to, I understand."

"No, I'd like that," I replied.

"Good. I'll check my schedule and let you know when I'm free, and from there we'll see if you can fit me into yours," he said.

"Sounds good."

"You still have my number?"

I nodded.

After he walked away, Lillian smirked. "Did he ask you out?"

"Yes, but, not for a date. Just to talk."

"That's still counts as one. Especially when a man looks at you the way he was."

"Oh? I hadn't noticed."

"Why would you? You're in mourning right now," said Dad, who'd also apparently overheard the conversation. "It's nice of him to offer an ear, but if he wants to turn this into something else, it's kind of tacky, if you ask me. Especially when you just lost your sister."

I told him about Dr. Price's sister and Dad's tune changed dramatically.

"Really? So, he understands what you're going through." Dad sighed. "You know, it's almost worse not knowing what happened to his sister. I hate to say this, but... at least we have closure with Brittany. We know she's not out there suffering anymore."

He was right in that aspect. The pain was still so raw, however, that the closure left me empty, bitter, and pining for justice.

Chapter 31

The Director

I WATCHED AS the small group left the hospital entrance. I'd learned about the twin's father, Rollin Halverson, ending up in the ER and wondered how he was fairing today. Especially after learning about Brittany. Her death was now all over the news and both Bear Creek and Summit Lake were in an uproar. The label "serial killer" was being thrown around, which I didn't particularly agree with.

I was an entrepreneur.

An artist.

A man with a vision.

Of course, I enjoyed my work, but wasn't that part of the American dream? Getting paid for doing what one loved?

I thought about my first kill and how uplifting it had been. The one that helped give me the courage to end Mother's life.

Jeffrey Bower.

Back in middle school, he'd bullied me constantly. From stealing my clothes in the locker room to picking fights with me whenever the chance presented itself, I couldn't catch a break from the guy. It had eventually stopped, but I never forgot the hell he'd put me through. One night, when we were both in the twelfth grade, I found him walking on the side of the road with a backpack. I offered him a ride and we went to a campground and shared the pineapple juice and rum he'd stolen from his parents. Of course, it didn't take long until we were both hammered. We started skipping rocks down by the lake and eventually started talking about the past. Instead of apologizing for being an asshole, however, he laughed about it and told me to let it go. To quit being a pussy. Something inside of me snapped and I hit him over the head with the bottle. We ended up in straight-up brawl and that's when I grabbed the broken handle from the rum and slashed his neck with the jagged end. I could still recall the blood pouring out of the wound as I watched the life flicker from his eyes. Instead of being scared, I'd found the experience empowering, freeing, and justified.

Fortunately, I'd had enough sense to remove the glass from his neck and drag his body into the marsh. Although the thick mass of cattails helped hide him for a while, Jeffrey was eventually found. Thankfully, as luck would have it, I was never connected to his death.

From that moment on, I was no longer afraid of anyone. I knew I had the power to snuff out those who threatened me. And... I did. Eventually, I learned on the Dark Web that I wasn't alone in my fascination with death. Others found pleasure in it too *and* were willing to pay for it. Of course, I didn't actually start making money on my kills until I was well into my twenties and knew how to hide my tracks.

My phone vibrated, interrupting my thoughts.

I took it out and noticed I had another email from one of the buyers. They were all getting frustrated. Of course, my own patience was wearing thin.

I needed to get the girl.

I needed to film the movie.

I need to fill my orders.

But, I also knew that rushing things was dangerous. That was when mistakes happened and *amateurs* ended up in prison. Not me.

Tapping on the steering wheel, I watched Whitney get into the white Caddy with her dad and another woman. A blonde. She too was interesting, but not the right choice for Marion. That role was already cast and I was determined to see it through.

Anxious about what to do next, I began following them.

Chapter 32

Whitney

AFTER ARRIVING AT the resort, I went with Dad and Lillian to their suite.

"Not bad," he said, stepping inside. His eyes swept over the room. "The cabin was better, but at least this is more secure."

"*And* the indoor pool is closer," Lillian added. She set her purse down on the sofa table. "Speaking of which, I'm thinking about going for a swim soon. Did you want to join me, Rolly?"

He grunted. "That's a big 'no' from me. You know I'm not a fan of community pools. Do you have any idea of how many kids pee in hotel pools? Swimming in it is not my idea of fun."

"That's why there's chlorine," Lillian said, taking off her coat.

"I don't care. You go ahead and swim your heart out. I have a lot of stuff to do, anyway." He sat down on the sofa and took out his cell phone.

"Really? Like what?" she asked.

He looked at her and frowned. "What do you mean, like what? Like finding out what the police and FBI are doing about Brittany's killer."

"Oh," she replied, turning red. "Yeah. I suppose that's a good idea."

He looked at his watch. "It's almost two. I'm going to also call *Montecristo's* and reserve us a table, if it's still possible. How does dinner at seven sound?"

"Works for me," Lillian said.

He looked at me. "I hope you'll be joining us."

I nodded.

"Good. Maybe you should try to get ahold of Rick and Joe. See if they'd like to as well? I know they had dinner there last night, but hopefully they won't mind returning."

"I'm sure they'd be fine with it. I'll try giving him a call," I replied.

Lillian checked her hair in the mirror and then picked up her purse. "I'm going down to the gift shop. I want to see if they have any swimsuits there."

"I believe they do," I replied, remembering that I'd seen several hanging up. They'd also had T-shirts, towels, and other souvenirs with the resort's name.

"Good. I wore the other one out in the French Riviera. It's been in my suitcase now and is starting to smell moldy. Like an idiot, I forgot to wash it out," she said, walking toward the doorway.

"Just throw it out and buy yourself a new one," Dad said. "Charge it to the room."

She turned and blew him a kiss. "Thanks, Rolly."

"No problem. Could you also pick me up something sweet? Anything chocolaty will do. You know what I like."

"Sure." She looked at me. "What about you, Whitney? Do you need anything?"

I told her I was fine.

"Okay. I'll be back," she said before heading out the door.

Dad leaned back in the sofa and rubbed his face. He then looked at me with deep sadness. "I still can't believe Britt is gone. What are we going to do without her?"

I sat down and leaned my head against his shoulder. "Honestly, Dad, I don't know either."

We reminisced about Brittany for a while, and soon we were both laughing and crying.

"There's so much to do," he said, wiping his tears. "Someone is going to have to inform her employer.

Not to mention, take care of her belongings and financial obligations."

"Don't worry, Dad. I'll help with all of that," I said, my chest tight. The future seemed so bleak without her. I still couldn't imagine a life without Brittany in it. It had been bad enough when Mom died. Now they were both gone.

"I know you will." He let out a weary sigh. "Then there's the funeral. I don't even know when they're going to release her after the autopsy."

"I'm sure the sheriff can get us the number to the morgue and we'll find out all of that stuff," I said, dabbing at my tears with a tissue.

"We should call him now. Is there a pen and paper anywhere?"

"Let me go and check on the desk," I said, standing up.

"Open up the curtains, too, will you? It's too nice of a day to keep them drawn."

"Sure." I walked over to the window and did what he asked. Staring outside, I noticed they had a view of the parking lot, instead of the lake.

I lowered my eyes and my heart skipped a beat. The silver Mercedes was parked in the lot. The same model and year as the one that had followed me.

"Do you have Sheriff Baldwin's number?" Dad asked from the sofa. "I can't seem to find his card."

"Uh, yeah, I do," I said, still staring at the car. This one looked like it had a license plate.

"Good. Don't forget the pen and paper."

I turned from the window, grabbed what he needed, and handed it to him.

"Dad, I'm going down to the parking lot for a minute. I left something in the car last night," I lied, still not wanting to tell him about the Mercedes. He'd never let me leave his side if he thought I was in danger.

"Okay. I'll start making my phone calls while you do that."

"Sure."

I grabbed my purse, hurried out the door, and took the elevator down to the lobby. As I walked out the front of the building, I dug my phone out, intending to take a picture of the Mercedes. That was when I noticed the vehicle's engine was running and it looked like two people were sitting inside. I quickly averted my eyes, missing what the couple looked like. I still wasn't sure if it was the same car, although it seemed rather odd that it would be back with the plates on it.

I walked toward the other side of the parking lot to my LaCrosse and went inside. Unfortunately, from my parking spot, I didn't have a good view of the Mercedes. As I was thinking about what to do next, my cell phone went off. Looking at the screen, I saw a message from my father indicating that we needed to drive to the morgue to I.D. Brittany's body.

The very idea made me sick, although I was also anxious to see her. Part of me held a spark of hope that the woman they'd found was someone else. Not my sister.

I told Dad I'd meet him down in the lobby and then put my phone away. Sighing, I got out of my car and headed back toward the hotel, glancing at the license plate on the Mercedes and memorizing it.

When I got back into the lobby, I quickly wrote down the number on a piece of paper and then walked over to the gift shop, to find Lillian. Not seeing her, I sat down in the lobby and waited for Dad. A few minutes later, he joined me.

"Did Lillian make it back to the suite?" I asked, standing up.

"Not yet," he replied. "Isn't she in the gift shop?"

I told him I hadn't seen her.

Frowning, he went inside to check for her himself and walked right back out. Stopping next to me, he texted Lillian and a few seconds later, she replied.

"She says she's checking out the pool area and should be here in a second. I'm going to leave the room key with her. She forgot to take one with her."

"Okay."

While we waited in the lobby, we both noticed the television screen above the fireplace where a newswoman was already reporting on Brittany's murder. I noticed it was the same journalist who'd tried interviewing us yesterday.

"The Bear Creek police say they do not have any confirmed suspects yet," the woman was saying. "But, some believe that this could be related to the Amber Simons murder, and…" she left a dramatic pause, "we just might have a serial killer in our midst. Back to you, Ray."

"Serial killer," Dad repeated and looked at me. "One who obviously travels, since there hasn't been any murders like this in Bear Creek or Summit Lake since that movie crew showed up. When did Rick say we could visit the set again?"

"Whenever we're ready," I said. "He just wants us to give him a call beforehand and he'll meet us on the set."

"Do you know the location where they're filming?"

"Yeah. He gave me the directions." I told him where it was.

He nodded. "Let's plan on going tomorrow."

"Fine by me."

He leaned back on the sofa and crossed his ankle over his knee. "I don't think Lillian's definition of 'hurrying' is the same as the rest of the world's," he said, looking at his watch.

I smiled.

"Oh." He slapped the top of the sofa cushion. "I forgot to tell you—Rocky sent me a text saying that a couple of FBI agents stopped by their place a short time ago and questioned them about the dinner they had with Brittany Friday night. I hope we get a chance to talk to them soon."

"Did Rocky mention if he learned anything new?"

"He didn't say."

Staring past him, I saw Lillian approaching from down the hallway. She looked winded.

"Hi. Sorry, it took me so long. Can you believe it? I actually got lost," she said, flopping down next to him on the sofa.

"You didn't find anything at the gift shop?" he asked, noticing her hands were empty.

"Honestly, I didn't find anything I liked," she replied. "Not to mention that most of the bathing suits were for larger sized women."

"So, I guess that means you didn't get any chocolate, either?" he pouted

Her eyes widened. "Oh, no. I'm sorry, Rolly. I totally forgot about it."

He patted his round belly. "That's okay. I definitely don't need to add this."

"Nonsense. Do you want me to get you something?" she asked, standing back up. "I can run in and grab you a candy bar or something."

"I'm seriously fine." He stood up and looked at me. "We need to get leaving now anyway. Ready?"

"Yes," I said, also getting to my feet.

He reached into his pocket and handed her the room key. "Here."

"Did you want me to tag along with you guys?" Lillian asked, taking it from him.

"No, Doll. You stay here. This is something we can do on our own," he replied. "*Should* do on our own."

She looked relieved. "Okay. What time are you returning?" she asked, putting the key card into her purse.

"I'm not sure. I'll send you a message later," he replied grimly.

"Okay. I'll probably go swimming then. Can you believe it? I forgot that I actually did pack a second swimsuit for the trip," Lillian said.

"There's been a lot going on. We're all scatterbrained right now," Dad replied.

She gave him a hug and a kiss and whispered something into his ear.

"Thank you," he replied, and hugged her again.

Lillian looked at me after he released her. "Are you sure you don't want me to join you? For moral support?"

"No, it's okay," I replied softly. "But, thank you." She nodded.

As much as I still wasn't too sure of the woman, I was glad Dad had someone to make life a little bearable at the moment.

THE MORGUE WAS in Bear Creek, so it was a little bit of a drive. When we arrived, the coroner was busy so we had to wait in the lobby for a while, where it was just the two of us. Fortunately, I guess.

"Did you ever notice these places have a strange smell?" Dad whispered, looking uncomfortable.

"I haven't really visited many of them."

"It's the same thing with funeral homes," he went on.

"Oh?"

"They both remind me of the smell of old books."

I raised my eyebrow. "Old books?"

"Yeah. Don't you think?"

I nodded. It did kind of smell like a musty, old house or library. What got to me was the deafening silence. Not that I'd expected music playing in the background, but it was eerily quiet, not to mention, sad and depressing. Being there reminded me of the reality of our situation and it put a lump in my throat.

Sighing, I leaned down and picked up a food magazine from the coffee table.

"You didn't get a chance to call Rick yet, did you?" he asked, as I began thumbing through the pages.

"No. I forgot," I said, looking at him. "I will on the way back."

"That's okay. I forgot to call *Montecristo's*, too. It's probably too late now. We'll just have to have dinner with them another night."

I nodded.

We sat there in silence and it felt like forever. When the coroner finally met with us, he asked if we preferred to identify Brittany by photo or to actually view her in person.

"I want to see her," Dad said softly.

"Me, too," I replied.

He brought us into a small room in the back, where she was covered by a white sheet. When we were ready, the coroner uncovered her face and my heart broke all over again.

"Is this your daughter?" he asked gently.

Dad nodded and reached over to touch her forehead. "Oh, God," he croaked and began to cry.

"I'm so sorry for your loss," the coroner said.

Still staring at Brittany, I grabbed Dad's hand, my own tears blurring my vision.

"Her hair is blonde," Dad said, as the coroner offered us a box of tissues. "I don't remember her mentioning that she'd bleached it recently."

"It's also short," I replied, frowning. "Very short. That's even stranger." Especially considering Brittany had never worn her hair above her shoulders. This cut and color wasn't her style at all.

"So, this isn't how she normally looked?" the coroner asked, taking notes.

"No," I replied.

"Okay," he said. "Her scalp did show signs that it was recently bleached."

"Has the autopsy been completed yet?" Dad asked.

"Yes. Because of the seriousness of the crime, we performed it soon after she arrived. The preliminary results will be released within twenty-four hours," he said.

I looked at the thick sheet covering her from the neck down. I shuddered to think of what she'd gone through in the killer's hands.

"Did she suffer much?" I asked quietly.

The coroner took a moment to answer. "I believe that she died fairly quickly from the first initial lacerations the perpetrator inflicted upon her."

"So, you're saying that the bastard stabbed her and she died right away?" Dad asked, wiping his tears.

He nodded. "I'll give you a moment alone with her, if you'd like," the coroner said. "Please don't uncover anything below the neck. Obviously, because of the autopsy and—"

"We understand," Dad cut in.

Nodding again, the coroner stepped out of the room.

"I love you, Britt," I whispered, touching her cool cheek. I leaned down and kissed her lightly on the forehead and then stepped back for Dad.

He leaned forward and also kissed her on the forehead. "Don't worry, baby girl," I heard him murmur. "We'll get this guy and make sure he pays for what he did to you. And if I get my way, he *will* suffer. I promise you that."

Chapter 33

Whitney

AFTER LEAVING THE coroner, we drove in somber silence to a funeral home in Summit Lake and made arrangements for Brittany. We'd decided to have her cremated and put into a tree urn. It was something she'd mentioned a while back, when death seemed like an eternity away.

"We'll plant her next to the apple trees in my backyard," Dad said sadly. "Remember how you used to play hide-and-seek back in the orchard when you were kids?"

"Yes."

I remembered a lot of things that had happened in the orchard, including the time we'd played truth-

or-dare with some of the neighbor boys, back in sixth grade. It had also been the first time she'd been kissed. I could still remember how we'd stayed up late into the night because she wouldn't stop talking about it. I'd been annoyed at the time, but now it was a memory I would have given anything to relive.

IT WAS AFTER six by the time we made it back to the hotel.

"I'll talk to Lillian and see what she wants to do about dinner," Dad said, sounding exhausted as we got off the elevator and onto our floor.

"Okay. I'd actually like to take a shower first, if you don't mind?"

"No problem. I could certainly use one myself," Dad replied.

We went our separate ways, and as I was getting ready for the shower, Dad sent me a text telling me that they'd decided to order room service and I was welcome to join them. I declined and told him that I wanted to get some rest, anyway. Especially since Rocky and I were going to Bear Creek later. Of course, I left that part out.

I made plans with Dad to meet them in the lobby around nine a.m. so we could drive together and visit the movie set.

Afterward, I took my shower and then decided to run downstairs to the gift shop. Although I wasn't much of a drinker, I'd seen a small bottle of wine in the cooler earlier. Now, it seemed to be calling out to me. I decided that after the last couple of days, I deserved a glass or two.

As I was paying for the Moscato, along with a ham-and-cheese croissant sandwich, I glanced out the gift shop at a man passing by. The guy looked so much like Vinnie, Lillian's ex, that I did a double-take.

"That will be twenty-one eighty-nine," the cashier said, getting my attention.

I paid for the items and left the store. As I was heading over to the elevators, I thought again about the man who'd looked like Vinnie, but then brushed it off. He'd also looked a little like Detective Parker. If anyone, it was him doing a little more investigative work.

Exhausted from the stress of the day, I went back to my room and poured myself a glass of wine. Sitting in the dark, I thought about Brittany and the times we'd shared together. By the time I finished the last sip, I was bawling my eyes out.

"Don't even think of having anymore," I could almost hear Britt saying as I considered another glass. "You're not going to be of any help if you're an emotional basket-case."

I laughed harshly. *Wasn't that the truth?*

I put the remaining bottle of wine into the refrigerator, scarfed down the sandwich, went into the bedroom, and set my alarm for nine p.m. I closed my eyes and fell asleep within a matter of minutes.

Chapter 34

Whitney

ROCKY PICKED ME up in front of the hotel at ten o'clock.

"Did you tell Jan what we were up to?" I asked after getting into the truck.

"Of course. You didn't tell your father, did you?"

"How'd you guess?"

"He'd be here. Right along with us."

I nodded.

THE DRIVE TO the *Top Shelf Saloon* took fifty minutes. It was almost like I'd imagined it to be.

An old dump.

The paint was peeling, there was graffiti everywhere, and the blinking sign needed bulbs. Instead of saying *Top Shelf Saloon*, it said *Top elf loon*.

"A biker bar, huh?" I said, noticing a line of motorcycles parked nearby. "Wonderful."

"Apparently. I don't usually come out this way. Hell, Jan and I don't even go to bars. She doesn't drink and I don't need to tempt her. Once in a while, I'll have a beer. But, that's it."

"I guess I never noticed," I replied as he parked the truck.

He explained that she'd stopped drinking cold turkey and used to have a problem with it back when she was married to her first husband.

"Good to know," I replied, remembering the times I'd almost purchased her wine for gifts. "So, are we going to survive this?"

He grunted. "Just don't look any of them directly in the eye and we should be safe. I hope."

I smirked.

When we stepped inside the bar, we found that it was karaoke night and pretty lively.

"Looks like we know why it's crowded," Rocky said. "It's not because of the ambience."

"Yeah."

Up on stage was a rough-looking guy in a biker vest singing *When The Night Comes*, by Joe Cocker. He looked like he was enjoying himself and the crowd around him was loving it as well.

"He's good," I said loudly as we approached the bar.

Rocky agreed.

"What can I get you, two?" the bartender asked, a woman sporting a tight, low-cut T-shirt, plenty of tattoos, and large hoop earrings. She was almost as hard-looking as the guy on stage.

Rocky ordered a beer and I settled on a Diet Coke.

"I don't know what we were thinking," Rocky said out of the side of his mouth after the bartender walked away. "Everyone *here* looks like a criminal."

He was right about that. Most of the guys had on the same patched vest as the singer and were definitely dangerous-looking. The women didn't look any less threatening.

"I have an idea," I said to him.

His eyebrow raised.

The bartender returned with his beer and my soda.

"Excuse me," I said, leaning forward. "Do you have karaoke *every* Monday night?"

"Yeah."

"Cool. That guy on stage is really good," I said.

She looked over at him and smiled. "Yeah, that's Leo. He's our bouncer. Everyone loves to hear him sing."

"I bet. So, I take it most of the people in here are your regulars?" I replied.

She gave me a funny look. "Yeah, why?"

Before I could answer, Rocky did for me.

"She's just curious as to whether you've noticed anyone, I don't know, *odd* hanging out here? Someone who may have rubbed you the wrong way?"

She laughed dryly. "All the time. Why?"

"My niece, her twin sister, was found murdered in town earlier today. We heard about that girl, Amber, who was also killed, and believed the two deaths are related."

I stared at him in surprise. So much for keeping a low cover.

The bartender's eyes grew round. "I heard about that. I'm so sorry for your loss," she said softly.

We both thanked her.

"You know, there have been a lot of people coming in here, asking about Amber. Mostly cops, of course. And, of course, the FBI," she said. "Do you know if they have any suspects for your sister's case?"

"No," he said. "And we're obviously very frustrated."

"Ah. So, that's why you're here. To see if you can do better at solving these cases?" she asked, looking amused.

"Maybe. We're just looking for answers," he replied. "The police don't seem to have any for us."

"Well, if you want answers, you can talk to Leo. He was here the night Amber was killed. He saw her leave. *Without* the boyfriend. Of course, Tommy has an alibi," she mumbled. "Not to mention he stole from the bar. I guess going to jail for murder scared him into confessing to the robbery."

"We heard about that," I replied.

"You know, Leo doesn't much like cops," she said, looking at the man on stage. "Not that he'd hide anything, but he might be more willing to talk to you when he finds out you're related to the girl found today. He's just sick about it."

"Yeah, us too," Rocky said sadly.

"We're all on edge. He has nieces and I have a daughter who just turned twenty-one," the woman said. "We want to find this asshole, too. You should talk to Leo."

"Can you set that up?" Rocky asked.

"Sure can. I'm his Ol' Lady," she said with a wink.

TEN MINUTES LATER, we were in the back with Leo, who was actually a very sweet guy, despite his fierce looks. After offering his condolences, he asked me a few questions about Brittany and then started talking about the night Amber was murdered.

"So, she left and refused a ride," Rocky stated. He looked at me. "Which means that she probably did walk home, or at least attempted to."

"Yeah, she was adamant about not wanting help from anyone. Almost like she was trying to prove to the world that she was a badass who could take care of herself," Leo said. "Damn, I just wish I would have followed her home anyway."

"You offered. Don't be so hard on yourself. She might have given you hell for following her," Rocky said.

"Yeah, well, at least she'd still be alive," he said in a grave voice.

"When Amber left, did anyone else follow her out?" I asked.

"I've been asked that numerous times. Unfortunately, I didn't notice if she was or not. I was helping other customers," he replied.

"Speaking of that, did you notice anyone new around that time?" Rocky asked.

"I did tell the police about one guy who was alone. He was from out of town, I guess. Had a Texas accent and cowboy hat. He seemed like a decent guy. Real polite."

"Did he pay by credit card?" I asked.

"No. He paid with cash. Was a big tipper, too," Leo replied.

"Has he been back?" Rocky asked.

"No. I only saw him that one night. Sorry, I don't even have a name for him."

"When did he leave the bar?" Rocky asked.

Leo shrugged. "Honestly, I'm not sure. It might have been after Tommy. I don't know, though."

"Was there anyone else in the bar that seemed 'off' to you?" I asked.

"You mean capable of butchering anyone?" he asked. "No. Not at all. Honestly, I think she was picked up while walking home. I keep thinking that the victim could have been Gina -my Ol' Lady. Or, her daughter. Hell, one of my *nieces*. Makes me sick. I keep running everything over in my head, wishing I'd done things differently. Including being more observant."

"Hindsight is always twenty-twenty," Rocky said, finishing his beer.

He nodded. "Yeah."

"Anything else you can remember about the cowboy?" Rocky asked.

"Actually, yeah. Now that you mention it—we had a hockey game going on earlier and I overheard him rooting for the Kings," he said, frowning. "I even gave him a little shit about it."

248

"The Kings?" I replied, not a hockey follower. "Where are they from?"

"L.A.," Rocky said grimly.

Chapter 35

Whitney

"L.A.," I REPEATED as Rocky and I left the bar. "This guy actually might be the killer. He also *might* be from California. Which also means that Dad's theory might be valid and the perp could actually be part of the movie crew."

"Maybe we should call his psychic friend and pick her brain some more."

I glanced at him, wondering if he was being glib. But, his face was serious. "I thought you didn't believe in that stuff?"

"Hey, when it comes to finding Brittany's murderer, I'm willing to try anything."

I agreed.

WE DIDN'T GET back to the hotel until almost one a.m.

"So, when are you all going to visit the set tomorrow?" Rocky asked me again. I'd told him about it on the way back.

"I'm meeting Dad and Lillian in the lobby at nine a.m."

"Okay. Jan and I will meet you there, too. She took the rest of the week off from work."

"Okay. Sounds good."

Rocky dropped me off and watched as I entered the hotel. Once I was inside, I saw his truck pulled away.

Yawning, I started walking toward the elevators and noticed a couple getting on ahead of me. I heard the woman laughing and flirting with the guy, so I slowed down to take the next one up. To give them some privacy. When I saw the face of the man she was with, I stopped dead in my tracks.

Rick.

As soon as the elevator doors began to close, he also noticed me. His smile fell and I could tell that he'd been caught doing something that Joe might not approve of.

Although I barely knew him, I felt sickened by the fact that Rick might be cheating on his husband.

I pressed the UP button and waited for the next elevator. When it arrived, I got on, and as soon as the doors closed, my phone buzzed. I knew without looking at it, who was messaging me.

Rick.

Rick: *Please don't mention seeing me tonight to Joe. We had an argument earlier and I just need some time away. The woman you saw me with is just a very good friend.*

I sent him a message back telling him that it wasn't any of my business and I wouldn't say anything.

Rick: *Thanks, dear. I knew you'd understand.*

Although his explanation seemed innocent enough, my gut was telling me that he wasn't being completely honest. I hoped that I was wrong. Regardless, it wasn't my business and I had my own problems to deal with.

Chapter 36

Whitney

AFTER TAKING THE nap earlier, I had a hard time falling asleep. All I could think about was visiting the movie set in the morning and figuring out who'd killed my sister. When I finally managed to doze off, I dreamed about being chased in the woods by a man wearing a cowboy hat and carrying a big machete. Just when he was about to slit my throat, I woke up with a jolt and didn't get back to sleep for another hour.

The next morning, I could barely open my eyes when the alarm sounded. After crawling out of bed, I took a quick shower and then slipped on a pair of black pants and a dark green sweater. I swept my hair up into a loose bun, applied a minimal amount of makeup, and went down to the lobby a few minutes early to grab a bite to eat from the gift shop. After purchasing a yogurt parfait and a bottle of Starbucks caramel-flavored coffee, I sat down in the lobby and waited for Dad and Lillian.

"Sorry, we're late," he said tersely and then gave Lillian a dirty look.

"I couldn't help it. Everything of mine was wrinkled and I can't meet anyone famous looking like I just rolled out of bed," she said, smiling apologetically. "You know more than anyone about that, am I right?"

"Actually, I've made my peace with wrinkles," I replied, realizing that I hadn't thought about ironing in the last few days. It just figured that it would have to take a tragedy like this to fix the problem.

"Seriously?" Dad asked, looking surprised himself.

I shrugged. "Yes. Life is too short, right?"

"True," Dad said. "And *that's* something I know more about than anyone. Now, let's go."

"Wait, I think there's a stain on my dress," Lillian pouted, trying to wipe something away that I couldn't see.

"No time to change. Besides, I see nothing. You look absolutely beautiful. Nobody will notice if there's a mark on your dress. Believe me," Dad said. "Now, let's go before Rocky has a fit and *his* blood pressure starts to raise, too."

He was right. Lillian looked like a million bucks. Every hair was in place, her makeup looked perfect, and the outfit she had on was obviously worth waiting for. At least from my father's standpoint. She had on a tight-fitting black wrap dress and designer stilettos that I knew she'd be regretting once we reached the set.

"It's fine. He knows we're running late. He's meeting us outside with Jan," I said. "Lillian, are you sure you want to wear those heels?"

"Yeah, those don't look comfortable. Not to mention that we'll be outdoors," Dad added.

She looked down. "I'll be fine. I can climb mountains in heels."

Right.

"Speaking of blood pressure, Dad, have you checked yours lately?" I asked.

"Yes. And I've been logging it in, like Dr. Price said. I also took my pills this morning. Like a good boy," he said proudly.

"Excellent. Have you heard anything from Sheriff Baldwin?" I replied.

His smile fell. "Not yet."

I sighed. "So, still no suspects?"

"Doesn't look like it," he mumbled as we walked out the front door.

Rocky was parked across from the valet stand. He waved when he saw us.

"We're not all going to fit in his truck," Dad said as we walked toward them. "We'll need to drive separately."

"Okay," I replied. "I'll ride with them."

"Hi, kiddo," Jan said when I got into the back of the truck's cab. "How are you?"

I put my seatbelt on. "Okay. Been better. Still wishing I was sleeping and this was just one big nightmare."

"I wish it was, too," she answered. "It's still so hard to believe that Brittany is really gone."

"I know," I said sadly.

She reached back and squeezed my hand. "Just remember that if you *ever* need anyone to talk to, I'm just a phone call away. Even if it's late and you can't sleep. Okay?"

I smiled gratefully. "Thanks, Jan. I really appreciate that."

Rocky cleared his throat. "Not to change the subject, but did you tell your father what we did last night?"

"Not yet. You know that he's going to be upset that we kept it from him," I replied.

"Yeah, but we did it for his own good," he answered.

"I know. Speaking of last night." I told them about seeing Rick with a woman.

"I guess that doesn't surprise me," he said. "They're from Hollywood. Sex and sin is all around them. Most celebrity couples don't survive any kind of long-term relationship."

"They're not celebrities," I said. "Rick works in Special Effects and Joe writes screenplays."

"Maybe so, but they're still part of that world," he replied.

"I just feel so bad for Joe," I said. "He seems like such a nice guy."

"They both seem very nice, but you don't know what happens behind closed doors," Rocky said.

He had a point.

THE LOCATION WHERE the film was currently being filmed was on some private property near the west side of Summit Lake. As Rick had stated, security was tight. I called him as we neared the area and he met us at the entrance in a black Dodge Ram. After the security guards let us through, we followed him down a long, winding dirt road to a gorgeous cabin on the lake.

"Wow. So, they're shooting a horror movie, huh? I wonder what it's about?" Jan asked, looking out the window.

"We'll find out soon enough," Rocky said, following Rick's truck to a field where several vehicles were parked, including trailers and semis.

After we parked, Rick greeted us warmly and then went over the ground rules—no talking while they were filming. No badgering the actors. And, no wandering off without permission.

"It's like a field trip," Rocky said, smiling. "Do we get nametags, too?"

Rick smiled. "I know. I know. You wouldn't believe the kind of trouble people get into while visiting our sets. The rules are obvious, but many times ignored. Anyway, they're shooting a scene right now where the heroine, played by Marlow Frost, is trying to get away from an evil spirit down by the boathouse. Of course, it won't make a lot of sense as to what's happening, because we won't be adding CGI until later."

"What's CGI?" Lillian asked.

"Computer-generated images. Special Effects," he replied.

"In other words, you haven't worked your magic yet?" Rocky said.

He smiled. "Exactly."

Rick led us past the cabin toward the lake, where the scene was taking place. They were in the middle of filming so we couldn't get close until the director called, "Cut!" Once the cameras stopped rolling, Rick brought us down for a closer look.

"Wow, I had no idea there'd be so many people here," Jan said.

There had to be close to forty people surrounding the scene. Rick quietly gave us a rundown of who-was-who, and what their roles were. There was the production team, the assistant directors, script supervisors, sound mixers, boom operators, gaffers, and of course, the camera crew. Then there were the makeup and hair stylists, costume designers, and prop people.

"Oh, my God, there's Jimmy Frank," Lillian gushed, grabbing my forearm and staring at the actor, who sat by one of the producers.

Rick looked toward the actor. "Yep. I'll see if I can introduce you later. He's been in a 'mood' today, which means he might not be approachable."

"So, what you're saying is he's kind of an asshole?" Dad asked quietly with a smirk.

Rick smiled. "You said it. Not me."

"Still, I would *love* to meet him," Lillian said, obviously star-struck. "What about Marlow Frost? Can we meet her, too?"

"She's definitely more approachable," he replied. "I'll see what I can do."

After introducing us to a handful of people on the set, the cameras began rolling again, so we had to be silent.

As we were watching them film, I felt someone staring at me. When I turned to see who it was, my eyes locked with Jimmy Frank's. He smiled for a second and then looked away.

I had to admit, the man was good-looking, but I'd once read in some magazine that not only was he arrogant and demanding, but rude to some of his fans. I didn't care one way or another if we actually met him, or any of the other actors. I had to admit, though, being on the set while they were filming was pretty neat.

After the next take, the director, Ned, called for a break, and that was when Rick walked us over and introduced us.

"Ned, this is the family I told you about," Rick said to him.

"Nice to meet you," he said, standing up. He was tall, towering over all of us, in fact, with black hair sprinkled with gray, light-brown eyes, and an engaging smile. Ned held his hand out to my father first. "Rollin, right?"

"Yes. Thank you for giving us this opportunity," Dad said. "We really appreciate it."

"Our pleasure. I'm so sorry for your loss. I can't imagine what you're all going through," he replied.

Pain passed through Dad's eyes. He thanked him and then introduced the rest of us.

When Ned and I shook hands, his eyes softened. "You're the twin," he said and then apologized right away. "Sorry, I didn't mean to bring up your sister again. That was rude of me."

"No. It's fine," I replied. "We want to talk about her. We want the entire town to talk about her."

"So, you can find her killer?" he replied.

I nodded.

"Have the police made any progress yet?" he asked.

"Nothing they've shared with us," Dad replied gruffly.

"Hopefully, that will change soon. If there's anything we can do to help, let me know," Ned said.

"Actually, we're staying at the same resort as many of your crew," Dad said. "We don't have much to go on right now, but if any of your staff remembers seeing her, it could really help with the case."

"Of course. I'm staying there myself. I heard she was at *Waverly's* the night she disappeared. What time was that?"

"We think around nine-thirty," I answered.

"Okay. Yeah, if I hear anything, I'll definitely let you know," he replied.

261

We talked a little more with him and then Ned excused himself. That was when Lillian asked again if we could meet Jimmy.

"It looks like he stepped away," Rick said, looking back to where the actor had been sitting before. "I'll introduce you to Marlow now, though."

Marlow Frost turned out to be a sweet woman. She even gave me a hug and said she'd been following the news and praying for our family.

"Thank you," I said, touched.

We talked for a little while longer and then Rick walked us up to the log cabin for a tour.

"Whose place is this?" I asked curiously as I removed my shoes by the front door.

"I don't know. We're renting it," he replied.

"The floors are heated," Dad said after removing his loafers. "That's gotta cost an arm and a leg with a place this size."

"Yeah, I'm sure. There's also an indoor pool, a sauna, and a gun range downstairs," Rick said.

"Wow. Is it for sale?" Lillian asked, walking over to the gorgeous stone fireplace and looking at the candles and other small props on the mantle.

"I'm not sure," Rick replied.

"I had no idea that there were cabins this ritzy here in Summit Lake," Lillian said, turning around. "Wouldn't it be nice to own one of these, Rolly?"

"Nice but… expensive. Anyway, I'm not looking for property right now," Dad replied. "And if so, this is way out of my price budget."

Lillian's smile faltered. "Maybe we could rent one sometime?"

"Honestly, after everything that's happened, I don't know if I'll want to return here for a very long time. No offense, Rocky," Dad said.

"None taken," Rocky said with a sad expression. "I'd feel the same way myself."

Chapter 37

Whitney

AFTER THE TOUR, we all agreed that the cabin was breathtaking.

"Thanks for walking us through the place. It's unbelievable," I said as we stood in the great room, which had a twenty-seven foot ceiling and large oversized windows overlooking the lake.

"It was my pleasure," he replied. "Is there anything else you guys want to see?"

"The gun range?" Rocky asked.

"I think it's been locked up," I heard Rick say I stared out the window and noticed Jimmy Frank walking toward the cabin.

"That's okay," Rocky replied.

"If you guys don't mind, I actually have to get back to work soon," Rick said, looking at the clock his phone. "I'm going to try to get out of here at a decent hour tonight."

"We understand and don't want to keep you any longer. Thanks for the tour and setting all of this up," Dad said. "You don't know how much this means to us."

"You're very welcome," he said, smiling. "I'm glad it brightened up your day a little."

"It definitely did," Dad replied.

As we were putting our shoes on, Jimmy walked inside.

"How was the tour?" he asked, smiling at all of us.

"Amazing," Lillian said quickly and then held out her hand. "Hi, I'm Lillian. It's so nice to meet you, Mr. Frank."

He shook her hand. "You, too."

Rick introduced the rest of us, and then Jimmy offered his condolences.

"I actually heard about it on the news," he said and looked at me. "They didn't mention anything about her having a twin. I imagine you two were pretty close?"

I nodded.

"She was very beautiful," he said softly. "Good luck on finding the person who did this."

We thanked him and then Lillian got her selfie.

"Well, he seemed pretty nice," she said as we were walking back toward our vehicles.

"Yeah," Rick said. "He has his moments."

"You don't like him very much, do you?" Dad said.

"It's not that I don't like him. I just don't have a lot of respect for a guy who was handed everything on a silver platter. Unlike the rest of us. His mother was in show business and pretty much paved the way for him in Hollywood."

"He's a good actor, though," Lillian said. "Regardless."

"For the roles he plays, he does just fine. There's not a lot of acting required in horror, though. At least that's my opinion," Rick said.

I could definitely feel a jealous vibe coming off of Rick when he talked about Jimmy. I wasn't sure what it was all about, either, considering that both men were successful and handsome.

We thanked Rick again, and then, as I was getting into Rocky's truck, he asked if he could have a word with me. Of course, I knew what it was about.

"I'll be right there," I said to Rocky.

"No problem," he replied.

"I just wanted to let you know that Joe and I made up this morning after our little squabble last night. He's actually supposed to be meeting me for lunch soon," Rick said when we were out of earshot of the others.

"You don't have to explain yourself," I assured him. "Couples fight. It's no big deal."

He smiled. "Yeah. I just know that it probably looked bad, me and her together. Not to mention that she was hammered, which was why I chaperoned her back to her room."

I nodded. "I understand."

"Anyway, I'd appreciate it if you didn't mention seeing me with Rhonda. She and I are just friends, but Joe has some insecurities and might get the wrong idea."

"Of course. Like I said, it's none of my business and I'm not one to gossip," I replied.

"Yeah, well, there'd be nothing to gossip about, anyway. We just went up to her room and talked."

"Okay," I replied as we stared at each other. It was obvious he was trying too hard to convince me, which made me realize there was definitely something going on. Yeah, I saw them flirting heavily with each other. But, it wasn't my business and I wouldn't say a word.

He smiled. "Anyway, let me know if you hear anything about your sister."

"I will."

"Stay safe."

"Thanks."

AS WE WERE driving away, Rocky wanted to know what Rick and I had talked about. I told him.

"He definitely sounds like he's covering something up. That's too bad. Hopefully, things will work out and Joe doesn't get hurt," Rocky said.

I agreed.

Jan asked us if we'd made any discoveries on the set.

"In other words, did anyone strike you as being a possible serial killer?" she asked, looking both amused and yet serious. I had a feeling she wasn't convinced that anyone we'd met was capable of murder.

"Personally, I couldn't tell. I would have liked to have spent more time there, but… it is what it is," Rocky said.

"What about you?" Jan asked, looking back at me.

"Nothing stood out for me. Of course, I don't expect that the killer would wave his arms or draw attention to himself," I said with a smirk.

"Probably not. I noticed something," Jan said and looked back at me again.

"What?" I asked.

"Jimmy Frank was paying you a lot of attention. I caught him staring at you a few times," she said.

"Really?" I replied. "I noticed him looking once."

"It was more than once. Let me tell you," she said, looking amused.

"That's because Whitney is a beautiful girl. He probably thought she'd go all fan-girl on him. But she didn't. Unlike Lillian," Rocky said. "I thought the girl was going to open up her dress and make him autograph her boob after she got her selfie."

Jan snorted and I laughed.

"I know she's been trying, but I still don't get what Rollin sees in Lillian," Jan said. "They have nothing in common."

"On the contrary. They both like spending his money," I said dryly.

"Rollin *has* to spend money. But he doesn't like it," Rocky corrected. "My brother always was a penny-pincher and I know that as soon as the nostalgia of dating a young, beautiful woman wears off, he's going to start protecting his wallet more and she's going to walk away. You just wait and see."

"What do you think about Lillian?" Jan asked.

"She's growing on me a little," I admitted. "But, I can't see them spending the rest of their lives together."

Jan also agreed.

Chapter 38

The Director

WITH ITCHY PALMS, I watched as the group drove down the dirt road, kicking up dust in their path. Unfortunately, I hadn't been able to get anywhere near Whitney in the past twenty-four hours. Not to mention that my own private life had interfered a little as well. I would try again later and hopefully, get her alone.

Chapter 39

Whitney

AS WE NEARED the resort, Jan and Rocky invited me over to their place for dinner.

"Sounds great," I said. "What time were you thinking?"

"We'll eat around six, but you can come over earlier, if you'd like. Let Rollin and Lillian know, too. They're invited as well," Jan said.

"I'll send him a text when I get home, too," Rocky said, looking back at me in the rearview mirror.

"Okay."

They dropped me off in front of the hotel and I waited for Dad and Lillian as they parked and joined me. After telling them about the dinner invitation,

271

Dad nodded his approval and then stated that he wanted to go back to the room and lie down. "I'm tired. I think it's the pills the doctor put me on. He raised my dosage."

"Keep checking your numbers," I reminded him.

He sighed. "Yes. I will."

"While you take a nap, I'm going to go for another swim," Lillian said as we headed toward the elevators. "Whitney, did you want to join me?"

Not being much of a swimmer myself, I declined again. "By the way, I'm impressed. You really did wear those heels like a boss," I said, surprised she hadn't complained about her feet hurting. Although she'd taken them off in the cabin, we'd hoofed quite a bit on the set, especially walking back and forth from the field, where we'd parked.

"I wear heels like some people wear tennis shoes," she replied with a smirk. "I could probably even beat Rolly in a race wearing them."

"I think a turtle could beat me, I'm so tired at the moment," he said, yawning.

We got on the elevator and Lillian pushed the button to go up.

"I'd better call the sheriff and see if he's found out anything new," I said, watching the numbers light up as the elevator moved.

"Yes. Let me know if he has. After I bitched him out yesterday, I doubt I'm at the top of his list for contacts."

"I'm sure he understands," I said. "And honestly, it had to be said." Personally, I also didn't think enough had been done to find my sister. I didn't blame the sheriff for her death, but I wasn't happy about the investigation.

Dad nodded.

The elevator doors opened up and we went into our separate suites. As I was kicking my shoes off, my phone rang.

It was Jack.

I hesitated to answer, but did so anyway.

"Whitney, I heard about your sister," he started off and then proceeded to give me his condolences. "Is there anything that I can do?"

"I might need some more time off from work," I said, warmed by the fact he wasn't calling about work. That he was offering his sympathies.

He was quiet for several seconds. "How much?"

I frowned. "I don't know yet. They're trying to find Britt's killer and I want to stay in Summit Lake until they do."

"Do they have any suspects?"

"Not yet."

He let out a sigh. "Then, hon, you know that it might take years to find the person who did it."

273

"I don't think it will," I replied. "Anyway, I'll let you know how things are going by the end of the week, okay?"

"Yes. Of course. Would you like me to meet you up there?"

Part of me ached for his comforting arms. The other part, the sensible side, knew it was a bad idea. "No. Thank you, though."

"You sure?"

"Yes. I'll be fine. How did Monday's trial go?"

We talked about his day in court and then eventually, we ran out of things to say.

"Listen, I don't want to sound like an insensitive asshole, but I don't know if we can afford to have you take more than two weeks off," Jack said, finally.

"I don't know if that's going to be enough time."

He was silent for a few seconds and then said, "I guess we'll just have to wait and see what happens."

"Yes."

AFTER HANGING UP, I grabbed a can of Diet Coke and fixed myself two packets of microwavable macaroni and cheese, which Brittany had purchased on her first day there. It was a cheap meal, but something we'd both enjoyed.

I sat down at the table and sighed. "Don't worry, Britt. We're going to find your killer and I'm not leaving until we do. Screw Jack."

Of course she didn't answer, but I somehow felt like she'd heard me and approved.

After finishing the meal, I called Sheriff Baldwin. Unfortunately, he didn't have any new updates or suspects.

"We went and visited the movie set today," I told him.

"How did that go?"

I gave him the rundown.

"Anyone give you a bad vibe?" the sheriff asked.

"No. Not really."

"What did you think of the director, Ned?" the sheriff asked.

"He seemed nice enough."

"It's public record, but don't repeat this—Ned was once arrested for domestic violence. It was a few years ago and the charges were dropped, though. Two years ago, another woman put a restraining order out against him. She claimed he'd been stalking her."

"You're kidding?" I asked, shocked.

Was *he* the one?

"The woman who had the restraining order against him was an ex-girlfriend. So, that doesn't really fit the pattern of who were looking for. But, it does make one pause, doesn't it?"

"Very much so," I replied, my heart beginning to race. "Is he single now?"

"He's not married. I don't know if he's dating anyone."

"Did you question him personally?"

"Yeah, but that was before I found out about the arrest record and restraining order. I'll be paying him another visit."

"He doesn't happen to be renting, or own, a silver Mercedes?" I asked, realizing that I'd forgotten to call him about the license plate.

"I don't know. Have you seen it around lately?"

As I told him about seeing the couple in the parking lot, I dug in my purse for the license plate number and gave it to him.

"Was it a Minnesota plate?"

"Yes," I replied.

He sighed. "I don't want to burst your bubble, but I doubt it's the same person. Why would he remove the plate and put it back on?"

"That's what I was kind of thinking. But, it doesn't hurt to look into it."

"I agree and I will definitely check it out. Oh, listen, I have another call coming in. I'll give you a jingle when I find out anything."

"Okay."

After hanging up, I began pacing around the suite, my mind going back to Ned. Not only was he also staying at the resort, he'd actually been accused of abusive behavior. Sure, the charges had been dropped, but what of the restraining order? As far as I was concerned, he was definitely at the top of the list of suspects. I just hoped that the FBI, and Sheriff Baldwin, would take a closer look at Ned. I would also bring it up to Dad and Rocky later, for their input.

I glanced at the clock and decided that the soda had made me too antsy. Restless, I decided to do something healthy with my energy. I went into the bedroom, put on a pair of shorts and a T-shirt, and then went in search of the fitness center. After following the signs, I learned that it was two floors above the indoor swimming pool, which I had yet to see for myself.

When I arrived, I found the fitness center empty, which didn't surprise me for an early Tuesday afternoon. I immediately headed over to the elliptical section, which had a great view of the pool area below, and climbed onto one of them. After entering my weight, and setting the timer, I began the workout.

Five minutes into it, I glanced down to the pool and noticed Lillian in the water, doing laps. After a few seconds, I turned my attention to the television and eventually got bored. I looked back down toward the pool and what I saw almost made me fall off the elliptical.

Lillian was at the edge of the pool, and standing above her, was Vinnie. He was fully dressed and from what it looked like, they were having a heated discussion.

Swearing, I got off the elliptical and headed toward the stairs, not knowing what to think.

Why in the hell was he even here?

I wanted to believe that he'd followed her to the resort and was trying to woo her back. But, that would mean she'd voluntarily given him her location.

As I headed down toward the pool, my gut told me that something was going on. Something my father would not approve of. I knew I had to get to the bottom of it before he went through any further pain.

By the time I entered the pool area, Vinnie was gone, but Lillian was still doing laps. I stormed over to where she was swimming and waited until she saw me. It didn't take long for her to notice that I was waiting for her.

"Hi," she said, swimming over. "What's up?"

Trying to remain calm, I asked what Vinnie was doing at the resort.

A look of panic flashed through her eyes. "What do you mean?"

"I was upstairs on the elliptical and saw you talking to him." She opened her mouth to protest and

278

I stopped her. "*Don't* even think about playing me for a fool. I'm not an idiot."

She stared at me for several seconds and then let out a ragged sigh. "He just wanted to talk. His mother is in the hospital and he's freaking out.'"

"Really? And so he drove all the way here for sympathy?"

Lillian glared at me. "You of all people should understand the pain of losing someone. He's worried sick about her. He thinks she's might die."

I was torn between wanting to believe her, for my dad's sake, and wanting to catch her in a lie. "What's wrong with his mother?"

"She has cancer," Lillian said.

"Terminal?"

"I guess so," she said, looking anxious again.

I crossed my arms and began tapping my foot. "Does Dad know he's here?"

Her eyes widened. "No. He wouldn't understand."

"And for good reason," I snapped.

"Look, there's nothing going on between me and Vinnie. In fact, he's leaving and going back to Michigan."

"Good," I said.

"Please, don't say anything to Rolly. This is all innocent and he wouldn't understand. Vinnie and I were so close once. We're more like brother and sister now. He just doesn't have anyone else to talk to."

This was beginning to remind me of the conversation I'd had with Rick.

"And he couldn't just call?"

She shrugged. "I guess not. Look, you're blowing this way out of proportion. *Nothing* is going on."

"Nothing is going on," I repeated angrily. "Maybe so, but, I'm not keeping this from my dad. He deserves to know what's going on even if it's *nothing*."

"Fine. You don't have to tell him. I will," she said, getting out of the water and grabbing a towel from a nearby chair.

"Just make sure you do. Do it before we head over to Rocky's for dinner. Otherwise, I will."

"Whatever." Turning away, Lillian wrapped the towel around her, walked over to the lockers, grabbed her stuff, and left without another word.

Chapter 40

Whitney

TOO ANGRY TO work out, I left the pool area and walked to the gift shop. Inside, I headed over to the books and picked out one that looked interesting. I had to get my mind off of everything that was going on, and since liquor wasn't my friend, I decided it would have to be fantasy. On the way to pay for it at the register, I also grabbed a Snickers bar.

After paying for the items, I walked out and saw Vinnie again. This time, he was heading out of the hotel lobby, looking more irritated than ever. Curious, I followed him outside and watched as he lit a cigarette and moved toward the parking lot.

"Hey," a voice said, startling me from behind.

I turned around and saw that it was the valet from the other night.

"Oh, hi. Working again, huh?" I said, turning back to watch where Vinnie was going.

"Yeah. Did you need your car brought around?"

"No, I was just coming out for some fresh air," I replied, shivering slightly. It was starting to snow and it had actually gotten colder outside since the morning. Not to mention that I was wearing shorts and a T-shirt.

"Did you ever find out who was following you the other night?" he asked.

I was about to answer him when I saw Vinnie approach a silver Mercedes and get in.

"You've got to be kidding me," I muttered angrily.

Vinnie had been the one following me?

The valet asked me another question, but I didn't hear the words coming from his mouth. My head felt like it was about to explode.

What in the hell was going on?

"I'm sorry," I said, turning around. "I have to go inside."

"No problem. You must be freezing your tail off."

I suddenly noticed the way he was looking at me and realized that the teenager might have a crush on me. It was kind of sweet. "Yeah. I am. See you around."

"Uh, yeah. See you around."

My mind returned to Vinnie and I grew hot again. I stepped back into the hotel and headed toward the elevators.

What else could Vinnie be capable of?

Brittany?

Amber?

He was an ex-con, but from what I'd heard, his illegal shenanigans had involved drugs and theft. Of course it didn't mean he hadn't ever murdered anyone.

Making up my mind, I took the elevator up to my floor and walked directly to Dad and Lillian's suite. I rapped on the door, and a few seconds later, my father answered.

"Uh, hi. Did you get a nap?" I asked, noticing that he looked exhausted.

His lips pursed together. "A little. Then Lillian woke me up and we got into an argument. Come on in," he said, moving out of my way.

"About what?"

"You know exactly about *what*," he replied as I closed the door behind me. "She told me you saw Vinnie, too."

Relieved that Lillian had at least come clean to Dad, I sighed. "Where is she?"

He waved his hand toward the bedroom. "Taking a shower."

"What exactly did she tell you?" I asked, walking over to the sofa. I sat down and looked up at him. I knew this had to be upsetting.

"That Vinnie's mother is very ill and he needed someone to console him," he muttered, staring off into space.

"Do you believe her?"

He sat down. "Actually, no."

I stared at him in surprise. "Really? Why not?"

"Because I did some checking on him last month. His mother died a few years ago," he said in a low voice. "So, it's a bunch of bull."

I swore.

"Don't tell me *you* actually believed her?" Dad asked, raising his eyebrow.

I shrugged. "I mean I wanted to. For your sake. But—"I leaned back against the plush cushion and closed my eyes"—I kind of thought she might be lying, too."

"Well, she was."

I opened my eyes. "Have you told her that you knew Vinnie's mother was dead?"

"No. I wanted to see how far she was willing to take this."

"But, why? Why don't you just get rid of her?" I said.

The look he gave me said everything. He loved Lillian.

"I need to tell you something," I said.

"What is it?"

I told him about being followed the other night and how I was pretty sure it was Vinnie. "Sheriff Baldwin will probably verify it soon here, too."

"Someone was following you and you didn't tell me? Why would you keep this from me?" he asked angrily.

"Because you have enough to worry about."

He scowled. "Don't leave me in the dark anymore. If something would have happened to you, I don't know what I would have done."

"I won't keep anything else a secret," I promised. "As long as we're on the subject. " I also told him about visiting the bar in Bear Creek with Rocky.

He glared at me. "I don't know who I'm pissed at more—you, Rocky, or Lillian. You've all been lying to me."

"Rocky and I didn't lie, Dad. We just didn't tell you everything."

"You kept things from me. That's just as bad."

"I know, you're right. We should have told you, but we were worried you'd get too stressed out."

"Let me worry about me and you just worry about being honest. Who am I going to trust if it isn't you and my brother?"

"I'm sorry, Dad," I said, overwhelmed with guilt. He was absolutely right.

"Just, don't keep anything else from me," he repeated. "Please."

"I won't. Oh, that reminds me." I told him what the sheriff had said about Ned.

Dad's eyebrows shot up. "Really? Now, that's something to look into."

"I agree, although this thing with Vinnie is weird, too. I don't trust either of them, Dad. You have to send Lillian packing. She can't be trusted."

He nodded sadly. "Yeah, I know. I'll take care of it as soon as she's out of the shower."

"Do you want me here?"

"No. I need to do this myself."

Chapter 41

Whitney

I WENT BACK to my suite and tried reading the book I'd purchased, but of course, I was too worried about my father, so it was impossible to concentrate.

Eventually, I gave up and put the book down. I then turned on the television and began flipping through the channels. Eventually, I settled on a documentary and watched it while waiting for my dad to get back to me.

THREE HOURS LATER, I woke up with a kink in my neck from falling sleeping on the sofa. Grumbling, I sat up, rubbed my neck a few times, and then sent Dad a message. He answered back, informing me that he'd kicked Lillian out of his hotel suite.

Dad: *It wasn't easy, but I knew it had to be done.*

He explained that she'd started crying until he told her he'd known about Vinnie's mother. At that point, she claimed Vinnie must have lied to her as well. Fortunately, Dad didn't really buy it and sent her packing.

Dad: *I knew I'd made the right decision when she tried leaving with my Rolex and the five thousand dollars I'd left in the safe.*

Shocked, but relieved he'd caught her, I praised his decision and then reminded him about dinner at Rocky and Jan's. Unfortunately, he tried backing out, explaining that he just wanted to be alone.

I called him.

"Dad, the best thing you can do right now is to be with your family."

"I know. I'm just not in the mood to talk about Lillian."

"We don't have to. Look, you're coming with me tonight. I'm not taking no for an answer. Besides, it's too dangerous for me to go by myself."

He sighed. "You just had to pull that out of your hat, didn't you?"

I smiled sadly. "We both know it's kind of true."

"Indeed, we do."

He agreed to stick with the original dinner plans and then told me he'd swing by my suite at five-thirty to pick me up.

"Sounds good."

We hung up, and it was then that I noticed I'd missed a call from Lillian. She'd also left me a message.

"Please, call me. I could really use someone to talk to," she said, sobbing during her message.

Sighing in exasperation, I hung up. Although I didn't want to have anything to do with her, I was curious as to what she was going to say, so I called her back.

"Oh, thank God," she said, crying again. "Can we talk? Please, I feel like I'm dying right now. Your dad doesn't want anything to do with me and I know you don't believe me, but... I really love him."

"That's why you tried taking the money and his Rolex?" I said dryly.

"It was an accident. I just grabbed what was in the safe without looking. Please, I don't want to lose Rolly."

"Then why are you hanging out with Vinnie?"

"He's been blackmailing me," she said. "He's a really bad guy, Whitney. I'm so scared."

"Maybe you should talk to the police if you're this frightened."

"I'm going to, but I don't want to do it alone. Please, meet me in the lobby."

"Did you tell my dad all of these things?"

"Yes, but he's so angry right now. He refuses to listen to anything I have to say."

I sighed. She sounded like she was really in trouble. "Okay. Fine. I'll be right down"

She sighed in relief. "Thank you."

I hung up, grabbed my purse and keys—in case she wanted me to take her to the police station—and left the hotel room. I took the elevator down and saw her standing by the front door, holding her suitcase and dabbing at her eyes. I had to admit, she looked pretty pitiful.

"Oh, thank God," she said as I approached. "I wasn't sure if you were coming or not."

"I almost didn't. So, where do you want to talk?"

"Can we go to your car? I don't want everyone staring at me while I bawl my eyes out," she said, turning away as an older couple walked by.

"Yeah. Sure."

We walked outside to where my car was parked. I unlocked the door and we both got in. I set my purse in the back seat and then turned to her. "Okay. So, what's this about Vinnie blackmailing you?"

Lillian reached into her purse and pulled out a gun. She pointed it at me. "*Don't* move."

I stared at her in horror. "What in the hell are you doing?"

She didn't answer.

The back door opened up and Vinnie jumped inside. He closed the door and also pulled out a gun of his own. "Listen very carefully, bitch. You're going to start the car and pull out of the parking lot, got it?" he growled.

"What's going on?" I asked.

"Shut up and do what you're told," Vinnie said, cocking his revolver. "Or you'll die and so will your old man."

Chapter 42

The Director

I'D JUST PULLED into the resort entrance, when I saw Whitney, and her father's girlfriend, walk out of the hotel lobby. The blonde looked like she'd been crying, which made me very curious.

I watched as both women went to the parking lot and got into a Buick LaCrosse. A short time later, a man ran up to the same car and jumped into the backseat.

I waited, wondering what was happening. Something told me the man in the backseat wasn't a planned guest.

About a minute later, Whitney started the car and the three left the parking lot. I decided to follow them.

Chapter 43

Whitney

"WHY ARE YOU doing this?" I asked as we headed down the road.

"*Why?* Because of money. Why else? Now, if you cooperate and not screw this up for us, you're going to live through this," Vinnie said. "But only if you do what you're told."

"Look, I have some money in my savings. We can drive to the bank and I'll get it out for you," I said. "No questions asked."

He snorted. "Really? How much?"

"Five grand."

"That's a nice down payment, but not nearly enough. This isn't about your money, anyway,

294

sweetheart. It's about Daddy's. He has the kind of cash we're talking about."

"How much is that?" I asked coldly.

"Five-hundred thousand big ones," Vinnie said with a smile in his voice.

My eyes widened. "He doesn't have that kind of money."

Vinnie grunted. "Yes, he does. Right, Lilly?"

"He will when he converts some of his assets into cash," she replied. She started naming off some of his investments, like she'd been personally going through his finances. "Not to mention that he has a huge life insurance policy that would have gone to me if you wouldn't have screwed it up."

"Excuse me?" I replied angrily. "Why in the hell do you think you'd get anything from him, especially his life insurance?"

"We were supposed to get married, but now that he knows about Vinnie, that's not going to happen. Which is why we're going with Plan B. We're holding you for ransom," she snapped.

Disgusted, I had to keep from reaching over and punching her in the face. But, she had a gun and I didn't know what the woman was really capable of. This was shocking enough.

"My dad would have never married you," I muttered.

"The hell he wouldn't have," she replied. "We were already planning on getting married in the Caribbean next summer."

"So, you were going to marry my father and then murder him?" I asked.

"Not right away," she replied and smiled. "But, yeah, eventually."

I clenched my teeth together.

"Take a right up here," Vinnie said.

"Where are we going?" I asked, putting my blinker on for the stop sign.

"We're switching vehicles soon. There's a rest stop not too far from here," he replied.

"You're not going to get away with this," I said. "Kidnappers always get caught. Especially the ones who demand ransoms. It never works out. So do yourself a favor and let me go."

"I don't think so. We've got everything covered. You just worry about keeping your pie-hole shut and your eyes on the road."

Pie-hole.

Grr…

I asked them about Brittany's murder.

"We don't know anything about that," Vince replied.

I looked over at Lillian.

"It's true. We're not involved," she said. "The person that did that is fucked up."

"That doesn't mean we won't kill if we have to," Vinnie said loudly. "Now, stop with the questions and just drive."

I glanced in the rearview mirror and noticed a vehicle behind me. I wondered if there was a way to somehow signal that I needed help. It then dawned on me that Vinnie and Lillian might hurt me, but they *needed* me alive. I just had to figure out a way to get the other driver's attention.

"Could you please be careful with that gun," I said to Lillian, who was cleaning some gunk from one of her nails and holding it haphazardly. "You're going to end up shooting me by accident."

"She's right. Give that to me," Vinnie said, holding out his hand.

Sighing, Lillian handed him her gun.

I noticed ahead of me that there was a bend coming and a plan began to form in my head. It would be dangerous, but worth the risk.

"Hey, slow down," Vinnie said as I pressed harder on the gas.

"What? We're fine," I said while secretly reaching down and unbuckling my seatbelt.

"You're going to take that turn too fast," he warned, getting angry.

Obviously, he was right. If we missed the turn, the car would surely hit the guardrail. It would cause a lot of damage. Someone was going to get hurt. I just had to make sure it wasn't me.

Vinnie held the gun up to my ear. "I said *slow down*!"

"Fine." I took my foot off the gas and steered the car closer to the edge of the road.

"Quit screwing around, Whitney," Vinnie snapped. "I mean it."

I watched the speedometer. When we reached forty miles per hour, I pushed open the door—which wasn't as easy as I'd imagined—and tumbled out.

Chapter 44

The Director

I WATCHED IN utter disbelief as Whitney leaped out of the car, landed in the grass, and rolled down the embankment. As that was happening, the LaCrosse slammed straight into the guardrail a few yards away.

Stunned, I stopped my car, pulled my hoodie up, and raced down to where Whitney was slowly getting to her feet.

"Are you okay?" I asked, keeping one eye on the other vehicle. The entire front end was smashed in and there was steaming coming out of the engine.

Not recognizing me yet, she stared toward the car. "I'm fine. We have to get out of here and call the police. They kidnapped me."

"Wow. Okay, let's get you out of here," I said.

She followed me, limping to my vehicle.

"Here, get in back and lie down," I said, opening up the rear door.

Whitney froze and stared up at me. Her eyes widened. "Joe? I didn't even realize it was you. You can actually *talk*?"

"Yeah. I'm deaf, not mute," I lied. "Rick just likes to do most of the talking." The truth was, he didn't know that I could speak either. Or hear. Or make films. My husband was clueless as to the things I was capable of. And, it was for his protection. He would never understand why I did what I did. Deep down, I knew if he found out, I'd have to kill him, and he was the only person I actually cared about. Our life together was almost perfect and gave me a sense of normalcy, which I needed. Just as much as I needed to make my movies and take pleasure in the things I knew nobody else would ever understand.

She looked a little confused, but then glanced over at the LaCrosse again. "Let's get out of here," she said, getting into the backseat.

I closed the door and quickly got into the front. Looking over at the other car, I noticed the man getting out of the backseat with his gun in hand.

"Hang on," I said. "Looks like they're alive."

I put my car in drive and quickly made a U-turn before tearing out of there.

Chapter 45

Whitney

I STILL COULDN'T believe it had actually worked.

Not only had I survived, jumping out of a moving car, but I was now safe. Sore, but safe.

"I tapped him on the shoulder.

He looked back at me over his shoulder.

"Do you have a phone?" Mine was still in the car.

As was my purse and wallet.

He shook his head NO in answer.

"We need to go to the police," I said, just as he turned his head back toward the road. I tapped him on the shoulder again and repeated myself when he looked at me.

Joe nodded.

Relieved that we were headed to safety, I closed my eyes and rubbed my forehead.

About a minute later, I felt the car start to slow down and opened my eyes. Noticing that Joe had pulled over to the side of the road, I tapped him on the shoulder again.

"What's going on?" I asked when he looked at me.

"I need something from the trunk," he explained.

Before I could ask him why it couldn't wait, he got out of the vehicle and went to the back of the car. Sighing, I waited, listening as he rummaged around for whatever it was that was so important. A short time later, I heard the trunk close and Joe walked around. Instead of getting into front seat, however he opened up the back door.

"What's going on?" I asked, staring at him in confusion.

Instead of answering me, he shoved a wet rag over my face and I realized, in horror, that there was a slightly sweet chemical scent to it. I tried struggling, but blacked out within seconds.

Chapter 46

The Director

HER CONSTANT TAPS on my shoulder had irritated the hell out of me. Thankfully, I had a bottle of chloroform in my tool bag.

After knocking her out, I quickly wrapped her wrists and ankles with duct tape. Noticing she was already coming back around, I also put a strip of it over her mouth so I wouldn't have to listen to her yap. Satisfied, I shut the door, got back in front, and took off toward Bear Creek.

Chapter 47

Whitney

I WOKE UP dizzy, nauseous, and confused, until I remembered Joe holding the rag over my face. Realizing that he'd also tied me up with duct tape, I began to panic. I didn't know what was happening or why he was doing something so horrible.

"Ah, you're back," he said, glancing at me over the seat. "Sorry about all of this. It just works better this way."

Frustrated, I screamed under the duct tape.

"I suppose you're confused. Or, maybe you've figured it out by now?" he said wryly.

An image of Brittany came to me. Also bound in duct tape with this lunatic driving her somewhere.

Joe was the killer.

Obviously.

Was Rick also involved in this madness?

He looked back at me again and our eyes met. Joe smiled. "Yes, I see it in your eyes. You know what's going on. You're a crafty one. Your sister was, too. Which is why I need to be extra careful with you."

Tears filled my eyes as he confirmed what I'd suspected.

Joe had killed my sister.

"I didn't mean for Brittany to die the way that she did. In fact, I was going to let her go. But, she misbehaved and did something stupid."

What about Amber?

"If you don't give me any trouble, and play nice, things will work out for you in the end. I won't hurt you and you'll be set free."

I didn't believe him. I knew who he was. I could identify him. There was no way in hell he'd let me go.

"You're probably wondering why I'm even doing this. What's the purpose? Well, I'm remaking a movie. Part of it, anyway. I don't know if you've ever seen it, but it's the one with Janet Leigh and Anthony Perkins. Anyway, Brittany and I were in the process of shooting the shower scene when she tried to escape. Of course, things didn't go so well for her in the end. I just hope you're smarter than your sister and realize that there is no escape, and trying it will only end in pain."

The things he was saying made me sick.

This was all for some stupid movie?

He glanced back at me again and smiled. "Fortunately, your hair is lighter than Brittany's. I think we can skip the bleach this time. We do need to cut your hair, though."

I closed my eyes and cried, not for myself but for Brittany. I knew the maniac must have put her through hell before finally killing her.

"You women and your crying," I heard him say, a smile in his voice. "Most of you will sob over the drop of a hat. My mother was the exception. I never once saw her shed a single tear. Not even when I held the knife to her throat."

Joe kept talking the entire ride, telling me about his crazy mother who used to be an actress. She'd starred mostly in horror films, but had done a few commercials as well. The more he talked about her, the more I realized what had caused him to be psychotic, and everything came together. The woman had abused and tortured him for most of his life. He described one incident where she'd locked him up in the cellar, where there'd been rats, and how he'd cried all night, begging to be left out.

"The worst thing was that I kept nodding off and that's when the rats would creep closer. I still remember when one of them began nibbling on my hair. I can still remember the feel of its wiry fur as I batted it away, crying and shrieking for Mother. She, of course, ignored my screams."

He told me about other instances of abuse, like how she'd made him sleep on a box spring instead a mattress. He also hadn't been allowed to play with anything geared toward boys when he was really young.

"I learned at an early age that she'd wanted a girl. Apparently, I'd been her only disappointment in life. She made me play with dolls and tea sets and everything else you could imagine. Not to mention the times she would have me dress up in princess gowns. Of course, nobody else saw this happening. To the outside world, she was the perfect mother, and when we were in the public eye, she actually was," he said wistfully. "Those were the times that she actually did her best acting. Even I fell for it…"

If the man hadn't killed my sister, and God knows how many others, I may have felt sorry for him. Now, I just wanted to get out the restraints and claw his eyes out for what he'd done to Brittany. Just because he'd been abused didn't excuse his savagery.

"I once wanted to be a professional actor, too, you know. I used to star in plays growing up, and my drama teachers used to praise me. I managed to even get some of the lead roles. Mother claimed that it was because of who she was and the size of her donations to the school. She claimed that I was a shitty actor and nobody else would ever admit it," he said and laughed harshly. "The old bitch used to tell me that I only wanted to act to show her up and that it would bring me nothing but humiliation. In the end, I proved her otherwise. I mean, nobody would ever guess the things I'm capable of. Hell, even my manhood can act. Look at Amber," he laughed harshly. "She actually thought I wanted her."

Joe turned the radio on.

"Man, was she a great screamer, though. What about you, Whitney? Can you hit those high notes?"

I glared at him when he turned around.

Ignoring me, he looked back at the road. "See, that's why I do these movies—to make them better than the originals. Make them more realistic. I guess Mother was right in the sense that I wanted to outdo her. But, not just her. There were a lot of shitty actresses playing lead roles in most of the old horror movies. Seriously, *bad* actresses. And that's where I come in. I try and recreate scenes in some of the most iconic horror films of all times. My goal is to make the hair stand up on the back of my viewers' necks. I want them to look at the terror in my films and feel the madness…" he grinned. "I want them to believe that what's happening is real."

Which it most certainly was…

I looked back at Whitney again and she was still shooting me dirty looks.

"Okay," I said, turning the radio up. "We'll talk more later. I can see that you're not in the mood."

Chapter 48

The Director

WHEN WE ARRIVED at the farmhouse, I cut the duct tape from her ankles and ordered her out of the car. Of course, the moment her feet touched the ground, she turned and began to run away.

I took off after her and tackled her to the ground.

"You try this again, or anything else, I'll slit you from the neck down." I snapped, after flipping her over. "Got it?!"

She nodded quickly.

"I don't believe you do," I said, pulling her up from the ground roughly. I needed her to know, early on, that I wasn't screwing around so I clenched my fist and punched her hard in the stomach.

Whitney gasped in pain and doubled over.

I grabbed her hair and pulled her head back. "The next time, I'll use a knife instead of my knuckles," I said, staring into her teary eyes.

She stared at me in horror.

I let go of her hair and pulled her into the farmhouse. Once we were inside, I brought her downstairs and handcuffed her to one of the tall metal shelving units.

"I have some shit to do," I said, a feeling of dread in my stomach. For some reason, I felt like this wasn't going to go the way that I wanted. I began to wonder if I'd made a mistake with her, too. Trying to remain calm, I issued her another warning. "Don't even think about trying anything else."

Chapter 49

Whitney

I DIDN'T KNOW what else he thought I could do. I was handcuffed in his basement. I couldn't go anywhere unless I pulled the damn shelving unit with me.

Joe walked away. "Leave the duct tape on," he warned.

I struggled not to throw up. Not only had he hit me hard, but I was scared as hell.

Knowing I needed to get my head together so I could come up with a way to get myself out of this mess, I breathed in through my nose and tried to relax. Of course it wasn't easy. Especially since I knew what kind of a monster Joe was.

Trembling, I looked around. The basement was large and had a lot of what I presumed to be his 'props' scattered around. Pushed into one corner was some kind of hospital gurney. Next to it was a metal tray filled with surgical equipment. There was also a saw on the tray, and thinking that he might have used it on Amber or Brittany was terrifying.

Joe swore loudly and I heard him throw something across the room.

Flinching, I looked over and saw that he was having problems with the bathroom lighting fixture. I watched as he attempted to change the bulbs to try to get it to work. But, it still wouldn't switch on after he was finished.

Frustrated, he grabbed a couple of portable work lights and set them up around the bathroom floor. After aiming them where he wanted, he looked at me.

"Sometimes you just make do with what you have. Kind of like you, I guess." He looked at my head. "So, are you ready for your haircut?"

I gave him a dirty look.

Joe smirked. "I guess that's expected. I'll be right back," he said, before disappearing upstairs.

I quickly looked through the shelves for something that I could use as a weapon. Unfortunately, it was filled mostly with towels, rags, and miscellaneous cleaning supplies. Of course, spraying Lysol in his eyes was a good defense, but the bottle was too big. There would definitely be no element of surprise.

Joe returned shortly with a pair of scissors, a comb, a curling iron, and a spray bottle.

"I'm going to move you to the chair over there. You try anything, and I'll cut more than your lovely locks," he threatened before unlocking the handcuffs.

I looked over at the chair, which was next to the bathroom. I gauged how long it would take for me to reach the surgical tools if I tried making a run for it.

Joe grabbed my arm roughly and pulled me to the chair. He shoved me down hard and then handcuffed my hands together in front of me.

"Remember, I have a scissors and I'm not afraid to use them," he sneered.

I glared at him.

Ignoring me, he took my hair out of my bun and started combing it.

"This shouldn't take too long. We'll cut it and then I'll add some waves. It needs to be curled a little before you step into the shower. Just like Janet Leigh's. How does that sound?"

My eyes told him to go to hell.

He smiled again. "Your sister at least pretended to be nice. I guess we know who the smarter twin was."

Chapter 50

The Director

WHITNEY WAS ANGRY as hell and it amused me.

I'd decided to not even try to reassure her again that everything was going to work out for her. She was already plotting in her head of ways to escape. I could see it in her eyes.

Fortunately, she sat still for the haircut. When it was time to curl her hair, I had to turn my back for a second to plug it in. Of course, the moment I did that, she was out of the chair and racing toward the staircase. This time, however, she almost got away.

"Dammit!" I growled, grabbing her by the ankle.

She fell to her knees and then tried kicking me in the head. Fortunately, I was much stronger and managed to pull her all the way down without getting a sneaker to the face.

"You're not listening to me," I hissed, grabbing her by the hair and lifting her up. I pulled her over to the chair and grabbed the curling iron, which was already growing hot. I pressed it against her bare leg and was rewarded with a muffled scream along with the smell of burning flesh.

"One more move and I'll shove this where the sun doesn't shine," I threatened. "You'll see what real pain feels like."

Whitney closed her eyes and cried.

I looked at the iron and imagined the damage it could do. I almost wished that she would disobey me so we could test it out.

Chapter 51

Whitney

THE CURLING IRON had hurt like hell. I knew I couldn't give up, though. It was better to fight than to give up because I was going to die anyway. I just needed a better plan.

Joe started curling my hair and I sat there looking toward the bathroom. I knew he wanted me to take a shower and that was when he'd probably dress like the wacko character from Psycho. I'd seen the movie many years ago. Not to mention, they'd made a series about it on Netflix.

As I imagined the shower scene, an idea came to me. A way that I might be able to escape. Of course, I could also kill the both of us in the process. After the torture he'd put my sister through, I knew I'd rather die by my own hand than his…

"SO, WHAT ARE you secretly planning on trying now?" he asked after spending several minutes curling my hair. "Or… have you had enough?"

I looked away.

He leaned down and roughly turned my face toward his. Our eyes met and he smirked. "Guess what?"

I couldn't talk because of the duct tape, so I just stared at him.

"Your hair is done. Would you like to have a look?"

I glared at him.

He snorted. "Yeah. I figured as much. Fine. Let's get the costumes on and start filming."

AGAIN, I DIDN'T fight Joe. Instead, I followed orders and even disrobed in front of him, after he removed the handcuffs, without making an issue out of it. I knew none of this was about sex. It was about terror and torture. I was safe from him until the shower scene.

"Here," he said, handing me a robe.

I put the robe on and tied it.

"Go ahead and take the tape off of your mouth."

I removed the duct tape and winced.

"I'm sure you're still dying with questions for me."

I shrugged.

His eyebrow arched. "Not even one question?"

"Fine. Rick really has no idea about any of this?"

"No," he replied.

"Not even the farmhouse?"

He shook his head.

"You two obviously have a lot of secrets between you," I said.

"What's that supposed to mean?"

I wanted to hurt him. Tell him that I'd seen Rick with a woman. But this guy was truly psycho. It would mean another death if my plan didn't work.

"Nothing," I said.

He kicked my clothes away and then told me to get ready. "Do you know what to do?"

"No. You never gave me a script," I said dryly.

"You're going to walk slowly through the bathroom door, check your reflection in the mirror, turn on the shower, remove the robe, and step into the bathtub. Simple, right?"

I nodded.

"And try to get it right the first time. Once you're in the shower, your hair is going to be wet. I don't want to have to dry and style it again."

"Okay."

His eyes narrowed. "You're being awfully compliant. What are you up to?"

"Nothing. I'm not exactly armed, so what else can I do?" I said dully.

He stared at me hard for a few more seconds and then nodded. "Just remember, I went through this with your sister. If you are planning on trying to run, I am already prepared for it."

"I won't. Let's just get this over with."

"We will. As soon as I change."

Joe pulled out a plastic bag from one of the shelves. He took out a gray wig and an old fashioned dress.

"Now for my transformation. I was going to wait until you were in the shower to change into my costume, but that didn't work out well the last time," he said, unbuttoning his shirt.

I looked away as he undressed. When he was finished, I looked over and felt a shiver go through me. He looked so damn creepy dressed like an old woman. If that wasn't bad enough, he applied some bright red lipstick to his lips, making it even more disturbing.

"Now, let's get into places," he said, moving toward the camera directly facing the shower. "Go on over by the doorway. I want to make sure I have the right angle."

I walked over to the spot and looked back at him. "Is this where you want me?"

"Yeah. Hold on. I need to turn on the other cameras."

I waited.

When Joe was finished, he looked pleased. "This is going to be so good. I can't wait. Oh. One more thing." He walked over to me with a bottle of perfume. "Close your eyes. I'm going to spray some Chanel on you."

My eyes narrowed. "Why?"

"Because it was Mother's favorite," he said in an eerie voice.

The hair stood up on the back of my neck. "Shouldn't you be spraying it on yourself? You're the one dressed like an old lady."

"No. This is for you."

"Fine." I just wanted to get it over with.

I closed my eyes and felt the mist hit me both on the neck and lips.

I grimaced. "Thanks for that."

"Sorry. Now," he put the bottle of perfume down and looked me in the eye. "You're going to behave, right?"

I nodded.

"Good."

"Anything else I should know?"

His red lips curled into a garish smile. "Just don't forget to scream when the time is right."

"Gotcha."

"The louder the better. Especially when I open up the shower curtain."

I nodded again.

"Okay." Joe moved out of the camera's sight. "One. Two. Three. Action!"

Chapter 52

The Director

WHITNEY TURNED AWAY from me and slowly walked into the bathroom. I focused in on her as she checked her reflection in the mirror and then walked over to the shower. Just like I'd directed, she leaned down, turned on the water, and then waited for it to warm up.

Smiling, I waited for the next part. Knowing many of the male viewers were going to appreciate what was about to come. Whitney had a beautiful body and it was almost a shame that it would soon be mutilated. However, I believed that there was more beauty in death, especially when it was shared with others for a nice, healthy profit.

I watched in rapt attention as she removed the robe and let it drop to the floor.

"Good girl," I whispered as she stepped into the shower and gave the camera a quick peek of her front side. When the shower curtain closed, I quickly grabbed the butcher knife and felt the savage rush of anticipation. This was the moment I'd been waiting for. The calm before the perfect storm. The *pièce de résistance.*

Chapter 53

Whitney

MY WHOLE BODY shook as I got into the shower. Frightened that my plan wasn't going to work out, I started second-guessing what I'd come up with and almost lost the courage to even try it out. But then I saw a bottle of conditioner and it felt like a sign.

Torn between anticipation and dread, I pointed the showerhead away from me, pushed the bathtub plug down with my toe, and grabbed the bottle of conditioner. After slathering most of it onto my skin, I set the bottle back down on the shelf and waited.

Come on, you bastard.

The seconds ticked by and it seemed like forever before the curtain was finally shoved aside. But, when it did, I was ready.

Joe raised the butcher knife above him and I could see the feverish look in his eyes as he waited for my scream.

"Joe Walters! Hold on!" I called out instead.

Growling in the back of his throat, he lowered the knife. "Great, now we have to shoot this scene all over again. Dammit!"

Taking him by surprise, I grabbed his arm with both hands and pulled him into the tub with me. He tripped over the side and landed on his hands and knees with a big splash.

"You stupid, bitch!" he hollered.

I crawled over him to try and get out of the tub. In the process, he grabbed my leg, but my skin was too slippery, so he lost his grip.

I fell down hard onto the linoleum, scrambled over to the work-light he'd plugged into the wall earlier, and grabbed a hold of it.

"No!" he hollered, comprehending my next move.

I raised it into the air. "This is for Brittany."

"Wait!"

Ignoring him, I threw it into the tub. "Don't forget to scream, asshole!"

Joe shrieked as the electric current charged through the water and rippled through his body. Backing away, I smelled his flesh burn right before he took his last breath. Drawing my knees to my chest, I closed my eyes and began to cry.

Chapter 54

Christmas Eve
5:15 pm

IT WAS SNOWING as I pulled my car up to Rocky and Jan's old Victorian house and stared at the Christmas lights they'd put up. My chest felt heavy as I recalled the year before, when Brittany and I had driven there together and how much fun we'd had on the way up. It was going to be a difficult holiday for everyone. Just like Thanksgiving had been. I almost dreaded going inside.

Taking a deep breath, I got out of my new vehicle, a GMC Acadia, and grabbed the box of presents from the back. As I was walking toward the porch, the front door opened and a Golden Retriever came barreling out.

"Lacey! Get back here!" hollered Amanda, Jan's daughter.

The dog ignored her, raced around the snow for a moment, and then met me on sidewalk.

"Hi, Lacey." I laughed as she began sniffing me and the packages.

Amanda walked down the steps and grabbed her by the collar. "She is such a stinker. Do you need any help?"

"No, I'm fine. Thanks, though."

Rocky stepped out of the house and then hurried down by us. "Hi, honey. Let me take that." He grabbed the box out of my hands before I could even protest. "Watch your step. I put some salt on the sidewalk, but it's still a little slippery."

"Okay." I followed them into the house and Jan greeted me.

"How are you?" she asked, giving me a hug.

"Good," I replied. "Surviving."

She stepped back and gave me a concerned look. "I imagine. We're so glad you're here. Your father should be arriving soon, too."

"Good."

Amanda released Lacey and the dog raced over to me. Smiling, I leaned down and began petting her.

"I'll put these presents under the tree," Rocky said, setting the box down next to the familiar beautifully decorated seven-foot Balsam Fir.

"Okay. It's so festive in here," I said, staring at all of the Christmas decorations. As usual, there were lights everywhere, the fireplace was lined with colorful stockings, there was a small holiday village set up on the sofa table, and an animated three-foot high Santa Claus waved at everyone from the corner.

"Unfortunately, Lacey has been intrigued as well," Amanda said dryly. "She's already ruined a couple of stuffed reindeer, thinking they were chew toys."

"Oh, no," I said, smiling.

"She doesn't know any better," Jan said. "But I do and should have put them up higher. Anyway, how was the trip up here? Were the roads bad?"

It snowed the entire trip and had taken me longer than usual to get to Summit Lake. I'd actually left at three a.m. knowing it was supposed to be rough driving. "It was manageable. Where's Kevin?" I asked Amanda.

"He's in the kitchen helping to frost cookies," Jan said before turning around. "Which reminds me, I'd better check on him. He was getting more of the frosting in his mouth than on the cookies the last time I checked."

"Of course he was," Amanda said, shaking her head and smiling. "And I bet Grandma didn't protest too much."

"Of course not. That's your job. Grandmas are the good guys. Right next to Santa, of course," Jan replied, winking at me.

I laughed.

"Would you care for something to drink?" Rocky asked after unpacking the presents for me and sticking them under the tree. "We have some eggnog, tea, apple cider, and soda."

"I'd love some eggnog," I replied.

"I'll go and get you a glass," he said.

Amanda and I sat down in the living room. We hadn't seen each other since Brittany's funeral, which seemed like yesterday.

"How are things, really?" she asked quietly.

I let out a ragged sigh and told her that I'd been keeping myself busy, which was helping.

"I'm also working for a new law firm," I added.

"I heard that."

After returning home from the nightmare, I'd asked Jack for some extra time off and thought he'd understand. Especially after having been kidnapped myself. Unfortunately, his true colors shined through when I was told it wasn't feasible. That the firm needed me too much. So, I quit, which actually took a large amount of weight off of my shoulders, for several reasons. Not only did I get some time to mourn for Brittany, but I ended up finding another company fairly quickly. The pay was also better and my new boss was much more understanding.

"I don't know if you heard, but Sheriff Baldwin has retired," she told me.

"Really?" I hadn't seen him since the funeral either.

"He felt like a failure after what happened to you with Joe. That's what he told Rocky, anyway."

I thought back to the night Joe had kidnapped me. After electrocuting him, I called nine-one-one and then my dad, who'd been worried sick about me.

The local police and FBI showed up to the farmhouse first, followed by Sheriff Baldwin, Dad, and Rocky. After repeating the story several times, I was treated for the burn on my leg, and then released into Dad's care. In the end, they found evidence connecting Joe to Amber's murder, along with several other women, including his own mother's.

As for Rick, he'd been devastated by the news, claiming that he had no idea the kind of monster he'd been living with. I knew it to be true and told the police the same thing.

In regards to Lillian and Vinnie, they'd survived the car crash with minor injuries and had lied to the police about why they'd been in my car. The two had claimed I'd offered to give them a ride before crashing it and disappearing. Of course, the police found their weapons and eventually learned the truth from me. Now they were both in jail and awaiting trial for Kidnapping.

"The sheriff shouldn't blame himself. I certainly don't," I replied. "Who'd have known, right?"

"I agree."

The doorbell rang and Lacey started going crazy.

"That must be your dad," Amanda said as we both got up. She grabbed the dog's collar.

"I'll get the door," I said and then opened it. When I saw who was actually standing on the porch, I stared at him in surprise. "Dr. Price?"

"Trevor," he reminded me and smiled.

"Yeah, sorry. Come on in," I said, moving out of the way. I saw that he was holding a large holiday fruit basket in one hand and a bottle of wine in the other.

"I hope I'm not late. I had to stop by the hospital on the way over," he said as I closed the door.

I looked at Amanda, who had a funny smile on her face. I wondered if she'd known he'd been invited.

"No, you're not late," I replied. "I just got here myself."

"Let me take your coat," Amanda said, releasing Lacey.

"I can hold something," I added.

"Thank you." He set down the fruit basket, handed me the bottle of wine, and then unzipped his parka.

She took his coat and looked at me. "I'll take the wine into the kitchen, too, and let them know he's here."

"Okay." I handed her the bottle and she disappeared.

"Lots of holiday spirit in here," Trevor said, removing his boots and looking around. "Someone really loves the holidays."

"Yeah, Jan."

"I wish I could say the same. I didn't even put up a tree this year. I've been so busy at work."

"I haven't either," I admitted, thinking about my dreary condo. It was the first time ever for me. I just wasn't in the holiday spirit.

Jan, Rocky, Amanda, and Kevin walked out of the kitchen together and greeted Trevor.

"Can I get you something to drink?" Rocky asked, handing me my glass of eggnog.

"Sure," he replied. "What do you have?"

Rocky listed off the choices again. "Plus, the wine you brought."

"I'll just have what she's having," he told Rocky, nodding toward my glass.

"Sounds good," he replied. "We also have some snacks set up in the kitchen, away from Lacey. If you're hungry."

"I'm starving, actually. I just got off of work," he replied. "Thank you."

"Perfect. Jan made enough snacks for twenty people. Follow me," Rocky said.

Trevor excused himself and the two disappeared into the kitchen.

"Hi, Kevin," I said to Amanda's son, who was around ten. "I heard you were frosting cookies. Boy, they look good."

"Thanks. They taste good, too." He took a bite out of his cookie, which was loaded with colorful frosting. Lacey sat down in front of him and began begging.

"Don't get crumbs," Amanda warned.

"Lacey can eat them. Grandma said it's okay," he replied.

"Yes, I did. Not too many, though," Jan replied.

"Okay, Jan," I said, lowering my voice. "Why is Dr. Price here?"

She gave me an innocent look. "He told me that he usually stays home alone during Christmas Eve. So, I thought—why not invite him here? He's such a nice guy. And very good-looking, don't you think?"

Amanda snorted. "Here we go again."

"What is that supposed to mean?" Jan asked her.

"You. Playing matchmaker," she said in a low voice.

"He was already interested in her." She looked at me. "He's been asking about you in town. Every time I run into the guy."

That made me smile. "Really?"

"Yeah. So, I thought—why not? Anyway, I think he's just what the doctor ordered," Jan said winking. "Better yet, he *is* the doctor."

"I doubt my father is going to agree," I mused. "He's going to think we're monitoring his health again."

"Actually, Rollin has lost weight I heard. And… I believe Rocky mentioned he was seeing someone else."

"Really? He didn't tell me about it," I replied. We'd been talking almost every day on the phone. It surprised me that he hadn't said anything.

"He didn't offer the information to us, either. Rocky pried it out of him after Rollin came for a visit a couple of weeks ago."

"That's right." Dad had mentioned that he was considering buying a cabin in Summit Lake.

"Anyway, he looked really good," she said. "A lot healthier."

I hadn't seen Dad since the funeral, either. "Good. I can't wait to see him."

"Speaking of which, that might be your father right now," Jan said, looking out the window at some approaching headlights.

I started putting my boots back on. "I'll go and see if he needs help."

"Wait... it looks like he already *has* help," Jan mused.

Curious, I walked over to the window and saw there was a woman sitting next to him in the vehicle. He turned off the car, and a few seconds later, the two got out.

"Oh, my God, this one isn't a teenager," I said with a smile as he walked around the car and held her hand.

"Watch Lacey," Jan said, getting ready to open the door.

Amanda grabbed the dog's collar.

Jan opened the door. "Hi, Rollin. Merry Christmas!"

"Merry Christmas to you, too," Dad said, stomping his boots off on the porch. "By the way, this is Mary."

"Nice to meet you, Mary," Jan said and introduced herself.

"Thank you so much for inviting me over with Rollin," I heard the woman say.

"Of course. We love having you. Come on in out of the cold," Jan said, stepping out of the way.

Mary walked in first, smiling at me, Amanda, and Kevin. "Hello. Merry Christmas."

I smiled warmly at the woman. She was slender—possibly in her fifties, with a white bob and bright hazel eyes. "Merry, Christmas to you, too."

"Hello everyone," Dad said, stepping in after her. "Happy Holidays."

Jan had been right. Dad looked like he'd lost some weight and didn't appear so puffy in the face.

"Hi, Dad," I said, giving him a hug. "You look great."

"Thank you," he replied, kissing me on the cheek. "You're a sight for sore eyes."

We held each other longer than usual, both of us no doubt feeling the loss of Brittany over this particular holiday. Thanksgiving had been bad, but Christmas had been one of her favorite times of the year.

Clearing his throat, dad released me and then introduced each of us to Mary.

"It's very nice to meet you," I said to her. "How did you and Dad meet?"

She explained that it had been through a grief counseling group that both of them belonged to. She'd also lost a loved one earlier in the year. Her son.

I looked at Dad, who was removing his jacket. "I didn't know you joined anything like that. Good for you."

He smiled sadly. "Actually, it *has* been good for me. I've only been to a few meetings, but it's helping me deal with everything a little better. You should join one. I'm sure they have something like that near you."

I nodded. "Maybe."

After everyone had a drink and was settled in the living room, Mary began opening up and talking about her son, Brian, who'd died in a motorcycle accident. Fortunately, she seemed to be handling it pretty well and from the way my dad was staring at her, I knew Mary was the best thing that had happened to *him* in a while.

"You're looking great, Rollin," Trevor said, who was seated next to me. "I'm glad you're watching out for your health."

"Thanks to Mary. She's a yoga instructor," he said, smiling. "Let me tell you, she's been helping me to bend in ways I never knew I could."

Like appreciating a woman not half his age, I mused to myself.

Rocky opened up his mouth to say something, and there was a wicked glint in his eyes, which Jan also caught.

"Be careful," she warned him. "Little ears."

He laughed. "I was just going to say women often have that affect us, whether we like it or not. For instance, I've found that I actually enjoy eating broccoli now, and Brussels sprouts, because she forced me into it. I wouldn't have touched them with a ten-foot pole a couple of years ago."

"I know what you mean," Trevor said, chuckling. "Although, I have to force myself into eating

339

vegetables. When you're single and always on the run, eating healthy takes more work."

"Have you ever been married?" Jan asked.

"No," he replied.

"Neither has Whitney," Dad said. "I don't think she dates much, either."

I scowled at him. "I've been busy."

"You're too young to be that busy," Dad said. "You should get out and enjoy life more."

I wanted to tell him I'd tried that a couple of months ago, and lost a sister. But, he meant well and didn't deserve my PMS. Plus, it would have been cruel.

"You know, I'm going to be traveling to Michigan in a couple of weeks for a conference. Where exactly do you live? Maybe we could get together for dinner and a show, or something? Just as friends," he said, looking at my father.

"She lives in Fairmont," Dad said, smirking. "And she has plenty of friends. What she needs is a nice, romantic dinner—"

"Dad!" I said, my cheeks turning red. "Seriously, just stop."

He laughed.

"How far is Fairmont from Detroit?" Trevor asked, looking amused.

"About an hour away," I replied.

"Perfect. We should keep in touch. I mean, if you're not too busy. I'm going to be out there around January sixteenth. What do you say?"

I couldn't lie, I was definitely attracted to Trevor and the idea of getting together, even as friends, cause a warm thrill in my stomach. "That would be great."

He grinned. "Awesome. It will give me something to look forward to."

"Me, too," I said, meaning it.

The rest of the evening went very well, despite Brittany's absence. It seemed that having Trevor and Mary around definitely made the holiday less depressing.

After a fabulous dinner, we opened up some presents and then Jan sat down at her piano.

"Let's sing Christmas carols," she said, looking at Kevin. "What do you say?"

"Yes!" He sat down next to her and the two of them began to sing. Soon everyone else joined in, including Trevor.

"Wow, you have a great voice," I said to him when we finished singing *Joy To The World* as a group.

He blushed. "Thanks. My mother wanted me to be a singer. My father wanted me to be a doctor. Personally, I think I'm better at healing people than making their ears bleed."

We laughed.

341

"You must be very good if your mother tried pressuring you into be a performer. I don't want to embarrass you, but would you mind singing a song for us?" Jan asked.

"Mom," Amanda said. "Don't pressure the man."

"It's fine," Trevor said. "I don't mind."

"Thank you," Jan said, beaming a smile at him. "Can you play the piano, too? Or would you like me to do the honors?"

Trevor stood up. "I can do both. It will probably make me less nervous if I'm concentrating on the keys, anyway."

"You, nervous?" she replied, standing up to get out of his way. "I find that hard to believe."

"When you hear me sing, you'll know why. Don't say I didn't warn you," he joked.

She chuckled.

Trevor sat down. "Any special requests?" he asked, looking at me over his shoulder.

"Silent Night?" I replied. It had been Brittany's favorite and she'd made Jan sing it every Christmas Eve.

Dad and I looked at each other. He smiled sadly.

"Yes," Jan said. "We didn't do that one tonight yet. Please. Sing that one."

Trevor grinned. "One last chance to stop me from ruining this song for you forever."

"Oh, stop," Jan said, hitting him playfully on the shoulder. "You'll do great. I can tell already."

Laughing, his fingers began to move, and it was obvious he'd had quite a few piano lessons. Then he began to sing and his voice took my breath away. It was smooth, rich, and so very unexpected, that all of us just stared at him in amazement.

"Wow," Jan mouthed, looking at me.

I nodded.

Trevor continued singing and I imagined my sister with us, sighing in pleasure. She would have probably fallen in love with the guy, just for his voice. Of course, she would have noticed how handsome he was, too.

Stop thinking about me and enjoy the song, I could almost hear Brittany saying.

Letting out a shaky smile, I glanced over to see that Dad was tearing up, just like me. Our eyes met and he smiled.

When Trevor was finished, we all sat there for a second, still caught up in the beautiful moment.

"That bad you're speechless, huh?" Trevor said with a twinkle in his eyes. He looked at me. "Great, and I made you cry. Nice guest, huh?"

We all started laughing and complimenting him.

"That was incredible," Jan said, patting him on the shoulder gently. "I can see why your mother

343

wanted you to be a singer. You even brought me to tears. Of joy, of course."

"Thank you," he replied.

"I don't think I've ever heard that song sung so beautifully," I told him. "You truly have a gift."

He blushed and thanked her again.

"Yeah," Rocky said, wiping a few of his own tears. "That was great. Brittany would have loved it. It was her favorite song."

The rest of us agreed.

We talked him into playing a couple more songs, and then it started getting late.

"I suppose I should get going," Trevor said a short time later, when he and I were alone in the kitchen. "I have to work in the morning."

"You're working on Christmas?" I said. "That's too bad."

He shrugged. "It is what it is. I'm off at seven, though. I don't know what your plans are for Christmas day, but maybe we could get together after my shift?"

I smiled. "Yeah. I'd like that."

We made arrangements for him to pick me up at Rocky and Jan's as soon as he could get away from the hospital. Afterward, he told everyone that he had to leave.

"I'll walk you out," I said, wishing he could have stayed longer. He was making me feel less empty inside and I already couldn't wait to see him the following evening.

"Thanks," he said.

After saying his farewells, the two of us stepped out onto the porch.

"Hold up," he said, looking above our heads. "Wouldn't you know? Someone put a mistletoe out here."

I looked up. "So, they did.".

"May I?" he asked moving closer. He stared down into my eyes. "Just a friendly one, of course. Like our date in Michigan next month. Not to mention, dinner tomorrow. I certainly don't want to pressure you."

"I suppose a friendly kiss won't hurt," I replied, still very much attracted to him.

Trevor pulled me into his arms and kissed me lightly. Then it grew to something much more passionate. When we finally pulled apart, he began to apologize.

"Don't apologize," I said. "Unless you regret the kiss. I don't."

He looked relieved. "I definitely don't."

I smiled.

There was a knocking on the window behind us. We both turned to see Rocky, Dad, Jan, and Amanda smiling and giving us the thumbs-up.

"Oh, God," I said, blushing. "Sorry. They can be a little crazy."

"Your family is incredible," he said, pulling me into his arms again and giving me a hug. "And so are you."

My heart did a flip-flop. "Thanks. You're not so bad yourself."

He pulled away for a second and his eyes searched mine. "If I'm overstepping myself, let me know. I'm usually not this forward. There's just something about you that I haven't been able to get out of my mind."

"I'm not complaining," I said, pleased by his words. I had a good feeling about Trevor, and deep inside, I knew my sister would approve of him, too.

He kissed me on the nose and then let me go. "I'm looking forward to tomorrow. And next month in Michigan. And wherever else this might lead."

I smiled. "Me, too."

I followed him to his vehicle and shared one last kiss before he left. As I headed back to the porch, I looked up into the sky and saw a shooting star. It reminded me of my sister and wondered if it was a wink from her.

Smiling up at the starry night, I whispered, "Merry Christmas, Britt. Give Mom a big hug for me. I miss you both so much."

Another star twinkled, and my heart told me that they'd both heard me.

The End

Made in the USA
Las Vegas, NV
30 December 2021

39838749R00193